## THE VELVET FLEECE

When their mark in a Miami con drops dead, Silky figures it's time to head West to Hart City on the California coast. And since Rick is their point man, he gets the job of setting up the fix. It looks like a piece of cake, ripe for the serving. All he has to do is pose as the best friend of a rich young war widow's dead husband, and he's in. With the rubes in this town, Rick figures it's a cinch.

Of course, there's Silky's girlfriend, Tory, who's bored with the boss and only has eyes for Rick. She's supposed to be in Havana, but Tory is no fool. She's followed Rick out west. And how he's got his hands full trying to keep the widow and Tory apart, while working a con of his own, only this time he's going to try to con Silky...

# Lois Eby & John C. Fleming Bibliography
(1908-1998) (1906-1964)

*Novels:*

There's Always Tomorrow (Arcadia House, 1944)
The Case of the Malevolent Twin (Dutton; 1946; reprinted as
  *The Case of the Wicked Twin*, Mystery Novel Classic, 1946)
Blood Runs Cold (Dutton, 1946)
Hell Hath No Fury (Dutton, 1947)
The Velvet Fleece (Dutton, 1947; Dell, 1949)
Death Begs the Question (Abelard, 1952)

*Stories:*

"Follow Me..." (with John C. Fleming; *Street & Smith's
  Detective Story Magazine*, April 1944)
The Borrowed Life (Fleming only;
  *The Pursuit Detective Story Magazine #1*, Sept 1953)
Lead to Murder (Eby only; 77 *Sunset Strip*, July 1960)
Murder Baits the Trap (with John C. Fleming; *Mike Shayne Mystery
  Magazine*, June 1958)
The Suspicious Bride (with John C. Fleming; *Mike Shayne Mystery
  Magazine*, July 1959)

## Lois Eby

Star-Crossed Stallion (Dodd, 1954; as by Patrick Lawson)
Star-Crossed Stallion's Best Chance (Dodd, 1957; as by Patrick Lawson)
Patty Lynn, Daughter of the Rangers (Dodd, 1960; as by Patrick Lawson)
Patty Lynn at the Grand Canyon (Dodd, 1960; as by Patrick Lawson)
Marked for Adventure (Philadelphia, 1960; non-fiction)
More Than Courage (Whitman, 1960; non-fiction)
Shirley Temple (Monarch, 1962; non-fiction)
Dogs of the World (Whitman; 1965; non-fiction as by Patrick Lawson)
Nurse on Nightmare Island (Lancer, 1966; Gothic)

# The Velvet Fleece
••••••••••••••••••••••••
## Lois Eby & John C. Fleming

### Introduction by Curtis Evans

**Stark House Press • Eureka California**

THE VELVET FLEECE

Published by Stark House Press
1315 H Street
Eureka, CA 95501, USA
griffinskye3@sbcglobal.net
www.starkhousepress.com

THE VELVET FLEECE
Copyright © 1947 by Lois Eby and John C. Fleming and published by E. P. Dutton & Company Inc., New York. Copyright renewed October 21, 1974 by Lois Eby and John C. Chester.

Reprinted by permission of the agent on behalf of the heirs of Lois Eby and John C. Fleming. All rights reserved under International and Pan-American Copyright Conventions.

"Grift at Your Own Risk: Not All Fleeces Are Golden"
copyright © 2023 by Curtis Evans

ISBN: 979-8-88601-031-2

Cover and text design by Mark Shepard, shepgraphics.com
Proofreading by Bill Kelly

PUBLISHER'S NOTE:
This is a work of fiction. Names, characters, places and incidents are either the products of the author's imagination or used fictionally, and any resemblance to actual persons, living or dead, events or locales, is entirely coincidental.
Without limiting the rights under copyright reserved above, no part of this publication may be reproduced, stored, or introduced into a retrieval system or transmitted in any form or by any means (electronic, mechanical, photocopying, recording or otherwise) without the prior written permission of both the copyright owner and the above publisher of the book.

First Stark House Press Edition: June 2023

# 7

Grift at Your Own Risk:
Not All Fleeces Are Golden
by Curtis Evans

# 13

The Velvet Fleece
By Lois Eby &
John C. Fleming

# Grift at Your Own Risk:
## Not All Fleeces Are Golden

by Curtis Evans

Like Frederic Dannay and Manfred Bennington Lee of Ellery Queen fame, Lois Eby and John C. Fleming were first cousins (her father and his mother were siblings) who wrote crime fiction collaboratively, as well as mainstream fiction, although their output for the murder market was rather minute, running from *The Case of the Malevolent Twin* and *Blood Runs Cold* in 1946 through *Hell Hath No Fury* and *The Velvet Fleece* in 1947 to, belatedly, *Death Begs the Question* in 1952. By far the best known of their crime novels today is the odd man out in the quintet, the crime novel *The Velvet Fleece*, on account of the 1948 film adaptation of the book, entitled *Larceny*, starring John Payne, Joan Caulfield, Dan Duryea and Shelley Winters, which has won a new audience today due to its restoration and release on DVD by Kino Lorber in 2021. The Cinemaretro website, for example, when writing of *Larceny* praised the "romantic shenanigans ... clever crime plot and truly shady characters that drive this little low budget gem," which until its denouement is remarkably faithful to Eby's and Fleming's novel. A year after the release of the film, Dell reprinted an attractive paperback edition of *The Velvet Fleece* as part of its popular—and highly collectible—"mapback" series.

Both Lois Christine Eby and John Chester "Chet" Fleming were native small-town Indianans, Eby having been born on November 20, 1908 in Wabash (fewer than 9000 souls in 1910) and Fleming having been born on April 27, 1906 in Elkhart (fewer than 20,000 souls in 1910). When she was a young child Lois' family moved out to southern California, where her father bought a citrus farm. After attending the University of Southern California Lois became successively a film studio secretary and scriptwriter. In appearance a girl-next-door brunette with a winning smile, Lois is co-credited with the scripts for the 1937 screwball comedy *Too Many Wives* and Republic's 1938 western serial *The Lone Ranger*. After her collaborations with her cousin ended in 1952, she went on to write several series of children's books and pony books, as well as a fangirlish biography of Shirley Temple. Lois Eby never married or had children, residing in Los Angeles with her parents until their deaths (her father lived to be 101), then moving to Florida, where she passed away at Lakeland on September 3, 1998 at the age of eighty-nine—whether with *Larceny* still in her heart, we know not!

While his cousin headed for Hollywood, Chet Fleming for years remained behind in Elkhart, where his father, John C. Fleming, Sr., was one of town's most prominent doctors, serving until his death in 1941 as chief of staff of Elkhart General Hospital, for the erection of which he had been largely responsible. After studying creative writing at Columbia University (he had been one of the six male members of the twenty-two member Art Club at Elkhart High School), outgoing and personable Chet—5'11' and 180 pounds, with a ruddy complexion, brown hair and hazel eyes—spent a decade writing advertising copy before becoming president and general manager of "Chet Fleming's Motor Inn" in Elkhart in 1934. That same year Chet married attractive and elegant Charlotte Josephine Barger, a daughter of an Elkhart accountant, with whom he had a daughter, Jacqueline, in 1945, after he had returned from service during World War Two in the 530th Armored Infantry and the couple had moved out to LA. Lois and Chet would charmingly dedicate their second mystery, *Blood Runs Cold*, to the yet unborn "Jacquie" as follows:

Expectantly Dedicated to
LITTLE JACQUIE

Whether he be a he,
Or she be a she,
'Tis all right with us,
We'll still make a fuss.

Chet and Charlotte soon separated, however, with the latter returning to Elkhart to raise their daughter, and the former remaining in LA, writing crime fiction with his cousin and working in the film industry.

The estranged spouses later divorced and married other individuals, Charlotte, interestingly, to wedding artist Ted Drake, creator of the Notre Dame Fighting Irish's famed Leprechaun mascot and lead graphic designer on the beloved *Kukla, Fran and Ollie* Fifties television puppet show, whose death in his nineties in 2002 was covered in the *Chicago Tribune*. "Little Jacquie" took her popular stepfather Ted's surname, suggesting that she did not maintain a close relationship with her birth parent. Chet Fleming, who had no other children, died in Manhattan at the age of fifty-seven on January 31, 1964.

■ ■ ■

Dysfunctional personal relationships and faithless men certainly characterize the cousins' fourth and most famous novel, *The Velvet Fleece*, which concerns the devious machinations of a group of grifters determined to fleece a wealthy young California war window. My guess is that Chet Fleming supplied some of the story's grit. Its antihero is a handsome, devilish charmer named Rick Maxon, aka Rick Fagan. At the opening of the novel he and his boss Silky Gould, aka Silky Angelo, find it necessary to lam it, along with Silky's other henchmen Dice and Max, from Miami Beach, Florida and depart for safer turf in parochial Hart City, California, where resides aforementioned naïve, pious war widow, Deborah Clark (nee Owens), the lovely, red-headed daughter of the city manager, who seemingly is just waiting to get conned. (Thinks Rick after seeing Deborah's photo: "a slick raggle all right, lots of class.") While unhappily bedded down at the local YMCA chapter, Rick, whom his fellows facetiously have nicknamed the "Featherbed Kid," poses as a war buddy of Deborah's fallen husband and he soon has the shy redbird eating contentedly out of his hand. But there is problem with the picture in the fetching form of Silky's sultry moll Tory Pizarro, who is also intimately acquainted with Rick and prone to flying into jealous rages when she suspects Rick of involvement with other skirts—like this redheaded twist from Hart City. Rick soon finds he has let himself in for more than he bargained for with this latest grift.

Shortly after its publication the film rights to *The Velvet Fleece*, which one critic dubbed "another top-notcher" by the writing duo, were snapped up by Universal. The next year the book was filmed under the unimaginative but accurate enough title *Larceny*. Directed by George Sherman, best known for helming a multitude of B Westerns for Republic, and scripted by a team including the Oscar-nominated William Bowers, the film is quite entertaining, with some impressively shot sequences (especially the twenty minute dénouement), snappy dialogue and good performances all round from its quartet of principals: handsome heartthrob John Payne, coming off the heartwarming Christmas film *Miracle on 34th Street*, in his first noir performance as Rick; lovely blonde Joan Caulfield, coming off her ingénue turn in the superbly sinister mystery *The Unsuspected*, as Deborah; that redoubtable film louse Dan Duryea as Silky; and Shelley Winters, coming off her much praised supporting turn in the Oscar-winning drama *A Double Life*, as tempestuous Tory. It is also nice to see native Irish future Oscar nominee Dan O'Herlihy, familiar to me as an Eighties film villain from *Halloween III* and *Robocop*, pop up as subsidiary grifter Duke, aka Dice from the novel. Additionally *Larceny* boasts winning turns from Dorothy Hart, who co-starred in the noirs *The Naked City* and *Undertow*, and Patricia Alphin, as two more fetching females smitten with Rick.

While critics complained that Dan Duryea was underused in *Larceny* (though in fact his part is quite faithful to the novel), many avowed that a sexy Shelley Winters, in her first major "harridan" role, outright stole the show. In its notice of the film, the *Chicago News*, for example, dubbed Winters "Jean Harlow with dynamite." Certainly the actress cheekily spouts off some of the film's best lines (courtesy of the film's scripters, not the authors), such as:

*One of these days you're going to lose me to an usher (uttered to Silky after he orders her to get out and go see a movie).*

*Stop twisting my arm! People will think we're married.*

*The only babe you wouldn't make a play for is a bearded lady.*

*Come early: I need somebody strong to help me mash the potatoes.*

*It's such a long time since I murdered my mother (uttered to Rick when she is trying to remember the number of bullets her gun will hold).*

Although the one-liners are, for the most part, newly minted, the film adaptation of the novel is an uncommonly faithful one. (All crime writers should have been so lucky as Eby and Fleming.) At least, that is, until the denouement, about which I cannot go into detail, except to note that it is more believable than the novel's twisty conclusion. Does Rick get his comeuppance, or does he get redeemed by the love of a good woman? Read the book and see, then make sure that you watch the film (if you have not already seen it).

Loyal Stark House readers may discern, as I did, certain parallels between *The Velvet Fleece* and *Fallen Angel*, the crime novel by Marty Holland—pen name of Mary Hauenstein, a film studio secretary like Lois—that that was filmed in 1945 under the same title by Otto Preminger. (That novel likewise was reprinted this year by Stark House.) Both stories concern handsome, unscrupulous male con men who take advantage of the kindhearted naiveté of pious women. It seems not improbable to me that in writing *Fleece*, Lois Eby and Chet Fleming were influenced by Marty Holland's crime novel, their other efforts in the key of murder being more traditional tales of detection. (Lois Eby may well have even known Marty Holland, since they had both been employed during the Thirties as film studio typists.) But in any event, both books stand out as fine examples of feminine noir, tough writing somewhat softened in comparison with the pitiless, masculine James M. Cain variety, but still packing a punch inside its fleece-lined velvet glove.

—March 2023
Germantown, TN

··········································································

Curtis Evans received a PhD in American history in 1998. He is the author of *Masters of the "Humdrum" Mystery: Cecil John Charles Street, Freeman Wills Crofts, Alfred Walter Stewart and British Detective Fiction, 1920-1961* (2012) and most recently the editor of the Edgar nominated *Murder in the Closet: Essays on Queer Clues in Crime Fiction Before Stonewall* (2017) and, with Douglas G. Greene, the Richard Webb and Hugh Wheeler short crime fiction collection, *The Cases of Lieutenant Timothy Trant* (2019). He blogs on vintage crime fiction at The Passing Tramp.

# The Velvet Fleece
●●●●●●●●●●●●●●●●●●●●●●●●
## Lois Eby & John C. Fleming

*This book is fondly dedicated to our own family,
cross-section of the professional world:*
DR. BARNETT S. EBY, a minister.
DR. J. MILLARD FLEMING, a surgeon.
JAMES M. SPROAT, an attorney.
*Also their wives and progeny.*

## Chapter 1

A single venturing gull tipped snow white wings against the sky.

Below it the Westwind's glistening keel dipped with the restless swells. The sun threw the hull's white length into brilliant relief against the blue backdrop of Pacific. The old thrill went through me. She had class that boat. Twice the class of Silky's. And the sweetest lines you'd ever find outside a woman.

I turned away from the window, glanced at my watch. An hour yet. I was dressed early but I didn't mind. I was glad I'd made a point of white tie and tails. It felt good to be back in the old soup and fish after the siege of slacks and Hawaiian shirts in Hart City.

It felt like Miami again. I thought of our last morning there. The morning that started us on the big job in Hart City that put me where I am today.

It began no different from a lot of other mornings. We were staying at a ritzy hotel. The Surfton they called it. One of those gleaming miracles of cream-colored stone and chromium ribbons that blossomed along Collins on Miami Beach in the opulent Twenties. For miles in both directions the hotel commanded an inspiring view of shining beaches; indifferent palm trees leaned lazily with the wind, a pleasant wash of color, cream, rose and yellow. All this slept contentedly under a high-arched, blue and distant sky.

With only a confidential whisper of efficiency the elevator whisked us from the twelfth to the twenty-third floor. Noiselessly, our feet sank into the deep-piled, expensive, white carpet on our way to Walton Vanderlinde's suite.

I remember the maid, Paulette, who answered the door at Van's place. French. Been personal maid to Mrs. Van before she died, and old Van was soft when it came to firing servants. She was cuter than seven hundred dollars—and lonesome. She used to leave notes in the band of my Panama. "The moon will be nice tonight down by the Casino." The distance between the hall door and Van's study was always too short for her.

I remember Walton Vanderlinde was standing behind his desk when she opened the door, his big square body in immaculate white linen blocked against the wide panel of gleaming glass wall beyond which were miles of curving shoreline. I even remember his heavy fist with its enormous diamond, beating a thoughtful tom-tom on the desk as he studied something before him.

His frown cleared when he saw us. He had the friendly eagerness of a St. Bernard and the handclasp of a bear. "How are you, Mr. Gould! Mr. Maxon!"

I said I was fine. I lounged in my favorite chair, and Van passed the Havanas.

Silky said, "Touch of neuritis again but I'll get some sun this afternoon and a rubdown."

"You've been saying that for three days," I jeered. I winked at Van.

"I'll steal an hour," Silky insisted. "But it's true. Things have been moving so fast...."

He handed the architect's drawings to Van. The big man spread them out on his desk. Silky lingered for a minute over the first one, the entire spread of building and bay labeled *Royal Yacht Club*, then turned on to the last drawing.

"The roof garden swimming pool," he said with satisfaction. "We've finally gotten Mr. Whitney's idea worked out, and the architect agrees it can be done. But he says it will be a miracle of engineering."

"Which won't hurt the Club any." I blew a smoke ring.

Van said, "It looks nice. Very nice."

Silky ran over the list of its features: the mirrored walls of the pool; the center fountain with colored lights playing over it; the tables and dance pavilion running around the pool; the tables done in pastel shades of crystal glass.

Van poured himself a glass of water. "Not too spry myself this morning," he apologized. He sat down as Silky went back to his chair. "Yes, it's a real layout all right."

"Keep this under your hat," I said. "Looks like we're going to sign up Paul Whiteman for the opening season."

"Fine."

"And by the way, an interesting cable came this morning." Silky's voice lowered with the weight of the announcement. "Another application for membership passed the board. Colonel Rittenhouse."

Van looked actually startled. "Of the British Intelligence?"

I chuckled. "Even the British Intelligence likes to relax."

"This Rittenhouse married the fifth cousin of the King of Sweden, I believe." Silky turned to me. "You knew him, didn't you, Rick?"

"Shipboard acquaintance, that's all," I said. "Last time I crossed on the *Ile de France*. Very nice chap."

It was then I noticed Van wasn't following me with his usual eager attentiveness. His big fist was moving up and down in its endless tom-tom on the desk. His square face was florid. He didn't look well.

I could see Silky was thinking the same thing. He said, "We'd better be running along. Just wanted you to see the pool." He smiled. "You know, I was skeptical of the idea when the Duke first suggested an International Yacht Club. But I'm beginning to be the biggest blow of all. I like the men you've put up, Van. We're getting the pick of sportsmen all over the world. I'm confident he'll be pleased with our progress."

Van passed across the blueprints. He was having trouble with his smile. He looked really sick. And his voice was hoarse. "Speaking of the Duke reminds me," he said. "I have a couple of pictures I want you to see." He handed Silky a snapshot.

Silky glanced at it and raised an eyebrow. "That's the snap I left with you. Of me on the Duke's cruiser."

"That's right." Van laughed. His laughter was hoarse too. He said, "I've had a kind of shock. I hope you can straighten it out."

My skin began to feel tight.

Silky said, "I thought you looked peaked."

"Last night I had a friend for dinner. He happened to see that snap. It puzzled him. This morning he sent me this." Van handed me an eight-by-ten glossy. I hoped he hadn't felt the coldness of my fingers in the transaction. I stared at the print and compared it with the snap. I whistled. "Isn't that the damnedest thing!"

Silky showed no astonishment when he looked at it. "From the size," he said, "I take it your friend was a photographer."

"An editor of one of Miami's papers. This print he remembered as one they hadn't used in the papers but kept in the files." He took a breath. He looked at Silky. "I've been comparing the two under a microscope. Everything seems peculiarly identical, the angles, the shadows, the cloud formations. Only one thing is different. In the glossy there is a strip of sky and a section of rail to the left of the Duke. In the snap, you are standing beside him."

Silky neatly pressed off the end of his cigar against the tray. "My snap was taken in Havana, Van, shadows and clouds to the contrary. So you can stop worrying. I'm not a ghost."

But Van didn't relax. He said, "I hope you're not a ghost, Mr. Gould. I hope to God you're who you say you are. Because I know it would be a comparatively easy matter to have this print slipped out of the paper files long enough to have a reprint made—a reprint superimposing your picture."

I exploded good-naturedly. I said, "Hey, what's going on here? Why would Mr. Gould do that?"

Silky was on his feet looking puzzled and pretty angry. He said quietly, "Yes, Van. I think explanations are in order."

The big man was trembling all over now. His face was kind of mottled. He said, "Believe me, I'll give a million outright to the Club if you can prove I'm wrong. But I'm afraid you can't. I've just realized I never bothered to check on you. You've been around here so long. I've played golf with you, cards, used your cars. Now a number of my friends have paid heavily for memberships in this yacht club. A club which, as yet, is nothing more than an option on a piece of shoreline, and this blueprint. I've heard of confidence men working in hotels...."

"Con man!" I began to laugh. I said, "This is choice! Wait till I tell Aunt Bertha in Santa Barbara I've been taken for a con man!"

But Silky was in a cold rage. He didn't shout, but his voice went through you like a knife. He said, "It didn't occur to me to pass out credentials, possibly because my integrity has never before been questioned." He leaned across the desk and pushed Vanderlinde's phone toward him.

"I don't intend to now. You would probably consider them forgeries. But I insist before we go any further that you call any or all the men I've mentioned and check on me. Call Mr. Whitney. Call Morgenthau. Call the Duke himself!"

Vanderlinde's gaze dropped before Silky's angry eyes. His breath was coming up through his great body in partial gasps. For a minute he seemed to deflate, to be slipping into shamed relief. Then a surge of fear tightened him. His square finger flexed against the speaking system. He answered the quick rasp of his secretary.

"Get me Whitney—Ja ..." and fell over his desk.

Before Silky or I could move, the secretary ran in, her eyes almost popping through her bifocals.

"Water!" she screamed at me.

She grabbed the ammonia from Van's top drawer. Silky called a doctor.

But it was too late. We knew in a couple of minutes it was all over. Walton Vanderlinde was dead.

The secretary began to cry. I gave her my handkerchief. She said the doctor had warned Van of a coronary occlusion. "Was he excited?"

Silky looked shattered. "No," he said. "Interested, perhaps too enthused over our plans." He patted the secretary's shoulder with a trembling hand. "Is there anything we can do? Anything? Perhaps notify someone?"

She said, "No." She said there was only his attorney and a son in South America.

I picked up the blueprints and the two pictures. The secretary took us to the door and thanked us.

She was crying again. "He was the kindest man!"

As we started down the corridor I heard the shrill scream of the French maid. She had been told. It was a damn shame.

Silky said, "What a break."

I agreed.

"Not that I couldn't have talked him out of it," he added

"I'd give ten years of my life," he told me, "to yell copper and let them throw the book at you for this."

The gun in Max Graber's hand lowered as the big ex-pug's eyes went over to Tory. His ugly face twisted and a sound like a hiccup worked its way up through his huge frame.

"Why don't we do that, Boss?" he pleaded.

"And have him stool on the mob to the first copper?" Silky snapped.

Max's voice rumbled in high outrage. "Well, if you think I'll help cover this thing for him...!"

"It makes my guts crawl," Silky agreed. "But we'll take care of him ourselves. He'll never get the chance to fink on us again."

Silky wasn't making jokes. I knew that. And the boys around me knew it. I could almost feel their silent approval. Believe me, I've been in some tight spots in my time, but this was the worst.

And it goes to show what training will do. Almost without knowing, I started talking.

"I don't know why you're so sore," I said to Silky in a voice so calm I marveled it could have come from me, "I did it in self-defense trying to carry out your orders."

I heard the sneers of all around me but I acted like I hadn't. I said, "I found her in my car in town. She wouldn't get out. Said I'd have to bring her home. Said she'd called Silky this morning and told him a pack of lies to make him sore at me."

Silky snarled. "Shut up! We're not suckers!"

"Any time you 'found her in your car,'" Max Graber sneered.

The dark little guy from Miami stuck a cigarette in his mouth. "That much *is* right, Chief," he said. "I saw her get in his car while it was parked in front of the travel agency. And he acted surprised when he saw her."

"Quiet!" Silky squelched him.

But it stopped him for a minute and I knew I'd had a break. I might have a chance now. A long one, but a hell of a lot more than I'd had the minute before. I went on in the same calm voice as if nobody had interrupted. I said, "I didn't want to be in on this play in the first place. And I didn't send for Tory...." Before anyone could start sneering on this one, I swung around to Max and put the bee on him. "Did I, Max?" I knew he'd have to answer me. He didn't know how much I knew about him and Tory.

Max gave me a venomous look. But he came through. "No," he said, "you didn't."

Silky turned his glare on Max.

I relaxed a little. I said, "I'm sorry you feel this way, Silky. Because I'd gone out to try and catch you at your hotel when I met Tory. To tell you the field is clear for the fix."

Silky reacted slightly to the magic words. I let them soak in. Then he got himself under control again. Before he could break the spell with his suspicions, I went on.

"You see, the Clark dame came to the Y this morning and told me she wanted to marry me."

He was watching me like a hawk, and the boys were watching him. He said dryly, "So we heard."

"That's what Tory was sore about. The Clark twist took me for granted, and ordered some wedding rags and Tory heard about it at the dress shop."

At the mention of Tory, I could feel them freeze again, but I was definitely better off than five minutes before. I tried a little offensive work. I frowned as if I couldn't understand their antagonism. I said, "I thought you'd be glad to hear about the Clark doll coming around."

Silky said, "Oh, sure. Sure. We *wanted* you to marry her for her three hundred grand."

God, Tory had talked all right!

I yelled angrily, "Marry her! Listen. Since when am I the broken-down has-been that needs to tie himself to a sucker for a few hundred G's. Couldn't I have had half-a-dozen widows in Miami with real money?"

"I told you to shut up!" Silky said violently. But his confusion was beginning to show now.

I said quietly, "Okay. Only I'd like to know what the hell you're grousing about?" I jerked my head back toward Tory. "I feel as lousy about this as you do. I liked the kid plenty. You know that. But you know the tales she could tell when she was riled. I don't see why we should let her spoil the game here just when we have it fixed."

The green light came on in Silky's eyes again. I let my voice warm with enthusiasm. "We could go through with it this morning. Deb's father is back. The play could be set up ..."

It was then the idea hit me. Probably the neatest con play ever pulled by a mob on a spot like we were then.

"We don't need the setup we worked out," I whispered. "We've got one now that will make a fix so airtight, the devil himself couldn't worm out of it."

Silky barked, "What do you mean?"

This was the acid test. If the idea didn't hit them right, I'd be stopping lead with my belly. Silky's left eye was twitching like it does when he gets excited. I took the plunge.

"We were hanging this graft rap on his daughter. Well—now we can make it murder."

I could almost feel them taking the shock of the idea. In the silence, my body went stiff, my eardrums tightened against the explosion of Max's Luger.

Then slowly Silky's lips moved in a reluctant murmur. "A setup all right."

Somewhere I found my breath again. Forced it in and out of my lungs in a semblance of rhythm. I knew I was out of it now. I had figured an angle Silky couldn't resist. I'd outsmarted the smartest con man in the business—anyway the next smartest.

The play began to fall into place.

"It couldn't have been better," I said. "Deb Clark found me with Tory. She hated her."

"I figured that out," Silky muttered.

I got a real breath this time. From now on it was a breeze. "Only her father knew how she felt," I said. "Which makes everything aces." My mind was all revved up now. I began outlining the play, and Silky was smart enough to give me my head.

When we had it set up, we told Max Graber to beat it to the first phone and call Deb.

"What do I tell her?" he growled. He wasn't happy about the way things were turning out but he wasn't crossing Silky.

Silky looked at me.

"Tell her you're a highway patrolman," I said, "and say there's a guy who says his name's Rick Fagan shot up out in a little shingle cottage on the beach. Give her the number—2265 Ocean Drive. Tell her this guy's calling for her."

Max repeated the message after me till he had it.

Then I gave Silky and the rest of the boys their orders, and explained to Silky what I'd do. It was some fun passing out the word once and watching Silky take it.

Only once did I have a bad minute. That was when I stooped to get my car keys where they'd fallen out of Tory's hand when I shot her. Her eyes were wide open—those grey-green glimmers of hers, and for a minute I had the feeling she was looking at me. It gave me a cold turn in the pit of my stomach. My hands were clammy around the key when I straightened again.

I started for the door.

Silky said, "Just to make sure you aren't pulling a fast one, Max and Louie will be right behind you with a persuader."

I didn't turn around. I wanted to get out of that house bad just then, out into the sunshine. I said, "Sure, I always like good company." And the door slammed behind me.

The seat of the Cadillac was hot from the sun. Max and Louie rode with me a couple of hundred yards to the clump of trees where they'd stashed their car.

"We'll be right behind you, big boy," Max said when they got out. He gave me a look. I was glad Louie was along. Max was the kind of monkey who'd be ready to go back to Silky and report the prisoner tried to get away, and let Silky take it on from there. But Louie would look ahead. Louie was practical. Louie wouldn't let his feelings run away with his judgment.

I drove back along the highway toward Hart City. It was only a little over an hour since I'd come along this road before. It seemed like a thousand years.

At the canyon road we'd decided on, I turned off. It was narrow and wooded. At the first sharp curve, about a hundred feet back from the highway, I U-turned and parked so that the Cadillac couldn't be spotted from the beach road but from where I could still see the highway.

Max swung in behind.

We sat there waiting.

It was a beautiful morning. Across the highway the sea sparkled under a flood of sunshine and I could hear the waves running along the shore. The canyon trees were alive with birds. A green, moist smell mingled with the smell of warm earth and salty ocean.

The hell of tension and grief and fear I'd been going through smoothed out all at once. I began to feel that old heady tingling that comes on me in the midst of a play.

And then I heard the train whistle. My watch said twelve-fifteen. It was the twelve-thirty train then. It waited in the station for fifteen minutes.

On that train, I thought, but for the grace of the devil, I would have been sitting now with Deborah Clark, waiting to go to Frisco and be joined with her in marriage and three hundred grand.

As though whipped up out of thin air at the thought, her Buick rounded a curve on the highway, speeding away from Hart City toward the fatal shingle cottage. Her hat was off, her hair was a red blaze in the sun.

All at once the perfect timing of the thing swept over me. Deb a hundred feet away … the train pulling in for a fifteen-minute stop at Hart City....

I could shoot out onto the highway, stop her car, race with her to the station, board that train just as it pulled out....

My heart began to pump like mad with that light, excited feeling I had the night I kissed her.

But a glance through the rearview mirror broke the dream. Max was leaning forward across the wheel watching, hoping. Max had been fond of Tory. He didn't like me today. And he was a crack shot with that Luger of his.

I sat still and let Deb's car flash on past the canyon road. I waited a full minute before I stepped on the starter and swung back onto the highway headed for Hart City.

## Chapter 17

I burst into Owens' reception room like a Kansas cyclone. The place was packed. The dopey secretary looked up and started to yam. I sailed right past her into Owens' private office.

He was busy talking to some palooka. He stopped and looked up at me, startled.

I was panting. "Have you seen Deb, Mr. Owens?"

He frowned at me. I was the louse who'd made his daughter unhappy last night. Deb evidently hadn't phoned him when she got my note. He said stiffly, "No, I haven't, Mr. Fagan."

"Thanks." I made it sound like, "God, I was afraid you hadn't!" turned and went out.

I figured this would be enough to throw him, he being in the state he was over Deb's health.

As the door slammed behind me, it cut off his call. "Is there something wrong?"

I didn't answer. I sprinted through the outer office and down the hall. Halfway to the elevator I heard his heels pounding after me. He just made it into the cage and the door clanged shut behind him. All the way down, he jabbered. I clamped my mouth shut hard and led him on a run to the Cadillac.

Max and Louie pulled out behind us.

I waited until we hit the Coastal Highway before I started giving him the tale. I underplayed it, watching his stiff, scared face out of the corner of my eye.

"Maybe I'm just nervous," I said. "I didn't mean to drag you away from your office...."

"What's happened to Deb!"

"I was supposed to pick her up at twelve-thirty, and she wasn't at home."

He shot me an incredulous look and began to relax. "Oh!" He wiped his face with a white linen handkerchief.

"Maybe she forgot the date," he said a little rebukingly. "You know how women are."

I said, "Women don't forget a date to get married."

He stared at me. "Married ...! She was going to marry you today?"

I nodded.

He was struggling to recover. His mouth opened to protest, question, then closed again. He said stiffly, "Maybe she had a last-minute errand."

"I hope so. But that girl, Tory—Deb told you about her...."

His voice sharpened with fear. "You mean Deb's with her?"

"That's what worries me. The girl's a devil. Came here to blackmail Deb. After I scared her into leaving town this morning, she admitted she'd already phoned Deb, threatened her if she married me she'd still hang around and blacken Jim's reputation."

Fear was riding him now—and digging in the spurs. Deb must have thrown a real fit last night over Tory. He was trembling. He said, thinking aloud, "Deb isn't herself since Jim died. Sometimes I think she's not quite—rational."

I nodded. "And Tory's no baby for a nervous girl to deal with."

He hunched forward on the seat as if urging the car faster. You could almost see the chamber of horrors his mind was throwing up.

"We'd better notify the police."

"If we don't find her out here," I said. "we will."

"You're going to that ... shack where Deb followed you last night?"

"Yes."

I could hear his hard breathing beside me as the dark circle of fir trees hove into view. Right now the place looked sinister even to me. Christ, what a buildup!

Deb's Buick was there all right. I wheeled into the driveway and parked behind it. And Owens couldn't help but see it. His face went a pasty grey. His hands, reaching for the door handle, were shaking. He was sure a soft slob when it came to that kitten of his.

He saw her first. I knew by his yell—a shrill, piercing scream like a wounded animal gives out. I jumped out after him, followed him across the sandy yard.

Sprawled at the bottom of the three porch steps was Deb's

body. She looked deader than hell.

Owens kept whining as we rolled her over on her face.

I had a bad minute myself. Then I saw she was breathing. "She's just knocked out," I said.

"Thank God!" He caught his breath and began to sob.

I pointed out a loose board in the sagging steps. "She must have stumbled," I said.

Owens' brain was sluggish but he began to get the drift I was shoving him toward.

"She must have been running fast to fall that hard...."

His eyes met mine and slid away. "Running away ..." they said silently.

He gathered her up in his arms and carried her inside to the couch.

He was frantically rubbing her arms and hands when his uneasy glance moved back around the room. I saw him wince as he spotted Tory's body.

She was sprawled on the faded carpet exactly as when I left, my gat still beside her. Owens saw it. He started breathing like a man under ether.

The boys had taken care of Deb all right. Now it was up to me. My role here was the frustrated lover. I clamped my hands beside my face and moaned.

"I won't let them hang this on her."

The words cut through Owens like a dose of hot lead. He sagged and muttered, "Hang...."

I rushed out into the kitchen, and brought in water and a towel, started bathing Deb's head. A second later I heard the heavy tread of feet crossing the wooden porch. The door opened and Silky and Max walked in.

At that minute I couldn't help but feel a certain admiration for the way Silky operated. His timing was always to the split second.

He said, straight and businesslike, "Is Tory Pizarro here?"

You could almost feel the waves of chill emanating from Owens. Silky moved his eyes quickly around the room. They stopped at Tory's sprawled body. Without a word he walked over to her, knelt down, drew a photograph from his pocket, made comparison, then straightened. "It's her all right, Joe," he said to Max.

I said, "Is she a friend of yours?"

A banal grin twisted Silky's lips. "Not exactly. She's got a record longer than a Congressional report. Right now she's wanted in fourteen states for buying hot goods." He shook his head wryly. "That gal was the fences' dream."

I put dread in my voice. "You're the F.B.I.?"

"Insurance investigator. Martin's the name." He extended his hand. I shook it. He said, "This is my assistant, Joe Banks." I nodded to Max.

Jesus! That Silky could act. Everything about him was perfect for the part: his conservative grey business suit; the slightly wavy, steel-grey hair; his ice-blue eyes, hard and sharp as diamonds, with a harried expression that guys get in the sucker rackets.

He slipped a fat Havana from his breast pocket and rolled it around in his mouth while he fired questions at us. He looked sympathetic when he heard Owens was Deb's father. But once we'd given him the layout, he added the thing up fast.

"She shot her, tried to make a run for it, and stumbled on that broken step."

He walked over to the couch and looked down at Deb's face. He sighed. "It's a shame. Looks like a nice girl. Probably just pushed too far. This Pizarro woman had a reputation for a nasty temper."

He gave Max a nod. "Stick around, Joe. See that nobody touches anything." He started for the door.

Owens moaned. But he didn't make any protests. I saw I'd have to carry the play.

I yelled, "Where you going?"

Silky paused. "To the local police. I don't see a phone around here."

I went into a berserk act. I pulled out every stop on the board. I yelled, "You can't do that. It'd be suicide to subject this girl to a murder trial. She's not well. That Tory was nothing but a tramp. She was pulling a blackmail scheme."

"I don't like it either, Mister," Silky shrugged. But...."

I shouted, "There's no justice in turning over a girl like Deb Clark to a bunch of dumb police."

I shot a glance at Owens. He was white and trembling. Through stiff lips he muttered, "There's no other way, Rick."

I cried, "There must be another way. I love Deb. We're planning to be married. I can't stand by while she's tortured to death...."

Silky laid a hand on my shoulder. "I can see your point, kid," he said. "But the law doesn't work that way. No matter how bad the Pizarro woman was or how good her killer, she's still been murdered."

Owens began to moan.

Silky said sympathetically. "It's a damn shame some of her underworld cronies didn't catch up with her before this happened."

"That's it," I shouted. "That's what I'm talking about. How do you know they didn't, and planted it on Deb?"

Owen's moans cut off short. He looked at me.

I put everything I had into it now. "If you get the police, circumstantial evidence alone will send Deb to the gas chamber."

Silky looked more sympathetic. But he said skeptically, "How do you think we'd keep it from the police?"

I looked around and said desperately, "All we'd have to do is get rid of that gun, maybe go over things for fingerprints." Silky looked at me as if I'd lost my mind. "That's suppressing important evidence. You know the penalty."

I cut in. I talked fast. "Nobody outside this room will ever know. Owens is city manager. We'll get Deb out of here. Then he'll order an investigation."

Owens was pacing the floor, wringing his hands and letting out half-audible sobs between his mutterings, "I know she didn't. My baby wouldn't do that—no matter how mad she got ... she's no murderess...."

I said sharply, "Mr. Owens!"

He stopped and looked at me dully. I took him by the arm and shook him to make sure he was hearing.

"You help me get Deb out of this, won't you? You'll cover with the local police."

He nodded slowly. "I'll help." he said.

The fix was in!

Silky took over. I had to hand it to him, knowing how much the game meant to him. There was no hint of elation in his voice, only anxiety and reluctance. He was pointing out all the trouble this might get him and Joe into. How he'd lose his job if it was ever discovered, maybe end up in the pen.

I had my breath by this time and went back to work. I didn't talk. I orated. I told Silky all of Owen's sterling qualities, his value to the town, his daughter's plans for the memorial, the utter worthlessness of Tory.

Owens was hardening like a good cement mix to the decision he'd made. He put in pleading grunts from time to time.

Silky looked at Max when I'd finished. "What do you think?"

Max hesitated. "Well, sometimes I do say private justice is warranted."

"I've never done such a thing in my life."

"I know," I cried. "But I don't see how you could sleep nights if you did otherwise in this case. Besides, there isn't too much danger. This Pizarro woman said she had no family. No one would ever bother to investigate."

Silky and Max finally came around. I could see the light in Silky's eye now. We had this little city manager over a barrel! He'd never dare to fink. We'd have a fix for as long as we wanted to operate around Hart City!

I got towels for us and we covered everything in the room for possible fingerprints.

Inside, I was boiling from the tension of the play. I gave Silky our old high sign that it was over. In the look that passed between us we said a lot of things. I'd pulled it off without a ripple. And I'd never be content to take orders from him again. I could tell he knew it too.

I shook his hand. "Thanks, Mr. Martin," I said. "You'll never regret what you've done today."

He said he certainly hoped I was right.

He started for the door.

And then from the direction of the couch came Deb's moan. Owens was at her side almost before it ended, running his fingers over her forehead. Color had begun seeping back into her face.

"Are you all right, Honey?"

She looked up at him, her glazed eyes bewildered.

He whispered, "You shouldn't have done it."

It didn't make sense to her. She turned her head till her eyes stopped on me. They were dull like they'd been that first day I went up to her house.

Her gaze stayed on me. The sight of me was bringing her out of it. In a minute that look was going to come back into her eyes again—that warm, lighted look. She'd cry, "Darling...." Hold out her arms....

And all at once I got that damned hollow feeling again. Christ! I had to keep hold of myself.

But it didn't happen. As the confusion cleared, a queer expression came into those eyes of hers. Without taking them off me, her hand groped out. Owens covered it with his.

When she spoke her voice was weak but clear. "Did it work, Dad?"

Owens said: "Just the way we planned, Honey. They had you framed for the murder. I was to incriminate myself by destroying the evidence."

The room seemed to stand still. Owens bending over Deb, Silky at the door, the goons behind him—figures in a diabolical frieze. A steel hand grabbed the nerves at the back of my neck and squeezed them into pulp.

And then Silky turned. His hatred of me seemed to leap from him. There was a rod in his hand.

"I should have known better than to let you handle a play, you dirty bastard! So you tried to rat on me ...!"

That heater was the only thing in the world to me right then. I saw his hand take a closer grip on it, his fingers tightened on the trigger. But I couldn't say anything. The words jammed in my throat.

And then from the blankness around me I heard the curt bark of command. "If you don't want murder added to the charges against you, *put down that gun.*"

It stopped Silky for a minute. When his eyes moved, mine

followed them.

The change in Owens was as great as the change in his voice. How the devil had we labeled this steel spring of a guy Milquetoast!

Not that it mattered. A hell of a lot of good it'd do him—or Deb either—now he'd blabbed and let Silky get the draw.

There was one chance. I took it. I looked Silky in the eye.

I said, "I'd do as he says, Silky. The place is surrounded by police."

Silky's eyes were venomous slits without reason or mercy. The rod in his hand moved up into place again—and stopped, as the sagging porch creaked under the pressure of running feet!

Owens looked at me. He smiled. "How did you know?" he said.

In a last glorious blaze the sun was dipping into the ocean now. The *Westwind* had stolen to the horizon's brink, the glow of light fanned over her in golden patterns.

There was just enough light to see my watch. The hour hand had been sliding right around. Not too long to wait now. I refolded my handkerchief. In a full dress like this you can't afford a bad detail to pull the eye away from the cut.

The door opened. But it was a stranger who came in. He shook my hand. He was pastor, he said, of Deborah Clark's church. He'd driven up from Hart City today.

"That's swell," I said. "Deb come with you?"

"No."

"Oh! Thought she might come up for the blowout tonight."

"No."

"Send me a message?"

"She asked me to come and talk to you."

"Swell. Give her my best, will you?" I told him what a choice dish I still considered her. "You weren't at the trial?"

"No."

"She really got herself some publicity. Afraid it'd be too much for her. She's all right?"

"She's all right."

"And give Charley my apologies—for underestimating him."

The guy looked confused.

I laughed. "Christ, when it came out *he* was the cookie who'd spotted me for a grifter and started Owens on that trip to Frisco to check on me! He and that watch trick he pulled on all 'questionable characters' to see if they were 'above temptation.' The little guy's terrific. He was born for the short con."

The minister said, "None of it was done in the spirit of bitterness or revenge. Neither Charley nor Owens nor Deborah...."

I patted his shoulder, chuckling. "I'm laughing at myself, pal," I said. "I had them all tabbed for small-town hicks, you know."

He nodded.

"I suppose you were with Owens, you and Charley both, the night Deb found me at Tory's and went home to cry on her old man's shoulder. That's the night the bunch of you gave her my history, wasn't it? And from then on she was acting under orders."

He nodded again, a little impatiently.

"Not a bad play you doped either," I said. "That little marriage gag stirred up hell all right, brought the mob out into the open. You've got imagination. Might see my way clear to let you in on the next job."

He didn't think this was funny. He said they hadn't allowed him much time. And wanted to know if I'd given much thought to this step I was about to take.

"Sure," I said. "You don't think I got this soup and fish without a petition? A lot of people are dropping in for the party, I'm told. The warden, several guys from the papers. Even the governor has tickets."

He said Deb had told him a lot about me that hadn't been mentioned in the trial. It was these things had brought him up today to tell me a story of another guy who'd lost his way and ended up on a third cross, but had repented and was given a last-minute reservation to Paradise.

He was a roper of the first water, this minister guy, smooth as they come. Acted like my welfare was all that mattered to him. And with a way of saying things that made them seem like the McCoy. All about human justice being of the letter, but divine justice of the spirit. "Time," he said, "has no validity on the books of God. A lifetime of sins can be erased in a second if the heart is cleansed—and heaven can be reached by every human soul who will face God in full acknowledgment and repentance...."

Deb must have really put the bee on him to send him on as long a drive as the one from Hart City to San Quentin! Cute raggle that one, sending her minister to plead for my soul. She was probably down there now in that room of hers with the ruffled curtains, praying for me! With that look in her eyes she'd had that night across the table at the Spa, telling me what my mother had said to me before she died....

And all of a sudden it happened again. That damned feeling that I was hollow as a balloon—that one soft word could prick me and I'd collapse. I sat there like a drowning man, hearing the minister's words going on and on. Warm, urgent, promising....

"... you've never imagined the joy you'll know once you've crossed the threshold into God's eternity with a pure heart ... once you've felt the peace of His forgiveness...."

Then, through his words, came the sound I had been expecting. The sound of footsteps along the hall. Moving like a slow precision hammer. Closer. Closer. The hollow feeling inside me expanded.

While the words beat at me in solemn command. "Try! You can do it, Fagan! You can throw off that identity you've been molded into. You can feel the freedom of humility, the glory of God's eternal pattern ... enter His kingdom of angelic peace ... eternal blessedness ...!"

The key turned in the lock. And with the sound, the cell around me took on shape. The minister leaning toward me in his mussed suit, looking hot and determined. I reached for a breath and loosed it through parched lungs.

The door swung open. In the narrow aperture, the jailer's boiled-potato face surveyed me impassively. "Ready?"

I stood up, straightened my tie, flicked an ash from my satin lapel.

The minister's fingers gripping my arm. I gave him a smile. "Thanks, mister," I said. "Tell the kid I'll be all right, see?" I shook his hand. "How can I miss? If this holy annex is as flush with suckers as you paint it, even a two-bit fink could clean. A big-time grifter like me ought to really be in the chips!"

We went out into the hall.

The door shut behind us with the crash of a drop forge, stamping hot steel.

THE END

Stark House introduces a new series...

# FILM NOIR CLASSICS

## THE PITFALL  Jay Dratler

"Dratler's novel is darker, sleazier and less forgiving than the film it inspired. A brutal portrait of blind lust and self-destruction... Dratler's *The Pitfall* deserves to known as a stellar example of 1940s American noir."—Cullen Gallagher, *Pulp Serenade*

Filmed in 1948 with Dick Powell, Lizabeth Scott, Jane Wyatt and Raymond Burr.

## FALLEN ANGEL  Marty Holland

"This story, about a small-time grifter who lands in a central California town and hooks up with a femme fatale, is straight out of the James M. Cain playbook."—Bill Ott, *Booklist*

Filmed in 1945 with Dana Andrews, Alice Faye and Linda Darnell.

Coming soon...
## HOLLOW TRIUMPH  Murray Forbes

"...a disturbed personality done in the noir tradition... an atmospheric and evocative yarn that spans the late 30s to through WWII."
—Amazon reader

Filmed in 1948 with Paul Henreid and Joan Bennett as *The Scar*.

**Stark House Press**, 1315 H Street, Eureka, CA 95501
greg@starkhousepress.com / www.StarkHousePress.com
Available from your local bookstore, or order direct via our website.

hastily.

"Sure," I yessed him. "He wouldn't have finished that phone call. He'd have felt too foolish."

"Sure. He was bluffing. But once a mark gets the jitters, you're never too sure when he'll blow his okus."

He took the two photographs from me, tore them into small pieces and dug them into the white sand in the alabaster jar as we waited for the elevator.

I tried to be philosophic about leaving Miami. I said, "I guess the cream is off here anyway for a while. After all, we took half a million last year. And this yacht club racket has cleaned us two hundred grand in memberships."

Silky raised his eyebrows. "What's eating you? We're not implicated in this. The girl was there."

"I don't mean Van," I said. "I mean that editor."

Silky scoffed. "Jerry will look him up and see he doesn't rumble. We have three good months here yet."

The elevator stopped at our floor. The doors started back as a siren shrieked below.

Silky said, "There's the meat wagon."

I got off and Silky went on down.

Dice was waiting in the apartment we shared. His coat was thrown across the satin bedspread. He was standing in the window, his long, nervous fingers pulling at the gaudy suspenders he always wore. He said, "What the hell happened?"

I told him the story.

He agreed with Silky it was a break, and we were set for a while here yet.

I said, "You and Silky are going soft. You're too comfortable here, and Silky's too damn fond of that Star Island estate."

"Where's Silky?"

"Gone over to see Jerry."

"Jerry will fix it. Jerry's a good fix. A big guy in town."

I poured myself a drink. It didn't touch the hard knot in the pit of my stomach. I said, "I think Silky's losing his grifter sense."

Dice let the cards he was shuffling drift slowly through his fingers. He looked at me surprised. "I think you're nuts."

"Vanderlinde's dying isn't going to help us. Silky shouldn't have let it happen."

"Yeah? And if you'd been top guy how'd you have prevented it?"

"Kidded him out of his suspicions without raising his blood pressure. Silky put on the screws too fast."

Dice went on shuffling the cards. "Silky's one of the smoothest operators in the business. I've worked with a lot of them. I know. Ever stopped to think what kind of a guy you must think you are to criticize him?"

"No," I said. "But maybe I should." I opened the top drawer of my dresser and began piling socks and shorts and ties out on the bed.

Dice frowned. "What're you doing?"

"Packing."

He gave me a derisive snort and called me a damn fool under his breath.

I went on packing.

After a half-hour or so, I could see it was beginning to get him. He was pulling aces from the bottom of the pack with savage flips. He said how long did it take Silky to talk to Jerry anyway? He said these were the times he wished he'd stayed a dip. He hated tension. He kept fretting and smoking and drinking, and dealing out the cards. After a while he turned his venom back on me.

"You're the one who's losing his grifter's sense! Steaming up when there's no heat turned on."

"It doesn't take some editors long to do that."

An ambulance went by and Dice winced at the siren. He had a fanatic aversion to prisons. He said, "You're only trying to undercut Silky again because of that dame. You're cutting off your nose. Silky's running the smoothest mob in the country. And he'll keep on running it. And don't worry about the fix. Silky has him primed and purring this time. Jerry has plenty of power in this town to fix a dozen editors and ..."

The phone rang. Dice's mouth stayed open. His jaw was set too tight to close it.

I picked up the receiver.

Silky's smooth tones came over. "Hello. Rick?"

"Yeah."

"Everything's fine, Rick. Want to drop out for a drink? I'm at home."

"Sure," I said.

I hung up the receiver. I said to Dice, "I was right, he's playing sunnybunny. The fix has curdled."

## Chapter 2

I went out to Star Island. Silky's Filipino houseboy let me in. I could see why Silky hated to give up the joint. He had leased it from some old Back Bay buzzard who must have spent his life collecting all the antique claptrap in it. It had a smell of elegance all right. And it gave Silky the chance to show off his pet accomplishment—a certain intimacy with more or less rare *objets d'art*.

Silky was on the terrace having a drink. He waved me to a chair and went on looking out over the three acres of lawn that stretched down to his private landing wharf. His boat rode at anchor a few hundred yards out, the gleaming white lines of its eighty-foot hull turned toward us.

The boy served my drink and left. Silky began to curse under his breath. I caught words like "... rat ... dirty phony ..."

I knew better than to get ahead of Silky, so I said innocently, "You mean the editor?"

"I mean Jerry," Silky ground out the words on his tongue. "Goddamned panty waist."

"What's his beef?"

"He says the guy with the glossy must have been the editor of the *Chronicle*. And he can't be fixed. He'll start raising holy hell once he hears Van's dead."

"He hasn't the pictures," I pointed out.

"I told him that. But he says it doesn't matter. The guy's that way with the new D. A., who's an ambitious slob. Jerry suspects he's collecting data on the mob, that he's even working on the dog tracks and our setup at Hialeah."

"In other words," I nodded, "Jerry is stopping the fix."

"After a year of the kind of dough he's been getting!"

"He's finicky now because he can afford to be," I reminded him. "He married a rich woman, joined the Sand and Surf and thinks he's smart in cutting loose from us." I sipped my drink and enjoyed Silky's running fire of curses. "Of course," I grinned, "he'd have been a hell of a lot smarter if he'd tipped us off to her dough, collected a cut, and not had to take unto himself a storm and strife."

"It proves what I've always said." Silky's fulminations had worked into the level of thought. "Money alone will never get you a strong fix."

"Uh huh." I showed no interest. I hated to start Silky on his favorite subject. Most big inside men have phobias of one sort or another as to the secret of success in the big con. Some are forever working out new games. A few do their own roping. But Silky's phobia was the fix. A strong fix, a right town was the formula he harped on. He'd been proud of this fix in Miami. That's why this had hit him so hard.

I said, "Do we blow today?"

"Yes."

"Right." I finished my drink and got up.

"Sit down," Silky snapped.

He rang the bell and the Filipino boy came out and brought us more drinks. Silky didn't say anything, but I could see he had stopped brooding over Jerry and was building up enthusiasm. That little secret smile of his he's so careful never to use in front of a mark was on his face.

"I've seen it coming for a long time," he said finally. "I've got a new town all laid out for us."

This was not bad news. We'd made a big take here, but I'd spent a lot too. A long layoff wouldn't have been too good. I said, "You mean the fix is already in?"

Silky gave me a funny look. "Not yet," he said. "But I've had a guy out there for a couple of months laying the foundation."

"How long will it take him to finish?"

He kept on looking at me and one of his eyebrows lifted over that smile of his. He said, "He's through with his part of it. From now on we take over—you and me."

I should have known it. A guy hangs on to an obsession long enough, like this of Silky's on the perfect fix, and sooner or later he's going to start experimenting. I didn't like it. I didn't like it at all.

Silky was wiping his mouth with the square of linen napkin he always serves with drinks, looking more and more pleased with himself. "I've worked out an angle," he said, "that's going to get us an airtight fix."

That was just what I was afraid of. When a guy starts talking in terms of perfection I always shy away. In one of the courses I took in a college once to help me hold my own with a bookworm mark, I read a piece by some Lord or Duke name of Dunsany, that said you didn't get the answers in this world. You just wondered about them. I went for that. A guy should dream but he shouldn't mix it in with his work.

I said, "Why don't we go up to St. Paul and kind of think this over for a while?"

But Silky didn't hear me. His eyes were looking like Columbus's must have looked when he saw that tree branch floating out from Cuba. He said, "It'll make history, this fix. It'll be in for the lifetime of the fixer. And what's more, the fixer needn't even get a cut of the take."

Now I knew he'd been hit too hard by this Miami thing. A big inside man like Silky lives under a lot of pressure. He wasn't the first who'd cracked.

"It's nothing new," he was going on. "It's been tried. But it's never been worked out right. That's what we're going to do." He looked at me again. "There's a dame angle to it," he said. "That's why I'm letting you in on it. You're such dynamite with dames."

I didn't like his smile too well now. I played it safe. I grinned like it was a joke and told him to quit kidding. This was the one thing standing between Silky and me—this twist, Tory. And it was enough. Silky had never caught us, but he knew. And the subject of dames was dangerous ground.

We got over it safely. Silky took a hard breath and gave me the setup.

He said the town he'd picked was Hart City, a small burg on the West Coast, a couple of hundred miles north of Los Angeles, a big tourist spot attracting the carriage trade from all over the country. He said it was a perfect sucker town, heavy with sugar yet they didn't even have a slot machine. It had never been organized.

I said, "Maybe there's a reason. Maybe the city fathers are hard to deal with."

Silky looked smug. "It doesn't matter," he said.

"Since when?"

"Since I decided our fixer is going to be the city manager."

I whistled. "Ambitious, aren't we?"

Silky brushed an ash from his yellow moleskin slacks. "How do you think I got this place—that yacht out there?" he said.

"By honest toil. By stashing your pennies in the bank and buying government bonds."

His smugness broke into a grin. He said, "As I told you, the setup is simple. This city manager is a soft apple, a widower, who's nuts about this kid of his. Your job is to meet her, turn on that famous charm, hypnotize her into taking part in a fraud game. Once we've got the evidence on her that will send her to the pen, her old man is going to play with us, and keep on playing."

"Blackmail is pretty strong medicine to pull before the fix is in," I said.

"It'll be a breeze the way I've planned it," Silky snapped. "Providing you aren't slipping with the dames."

I said, "As far as I know, I'm not."

He gave me a fast, sour look, but I didn't notice it. He said, "I'm cutting you in for five percent for the job."

I didn't get this one. Was he trying to freeze me out of the mob? I said, "Sorry, Silky. I'm a roper. I round up the sheep for you to slaughter. I guess I'll stick to my own work."

"You don't understand," Silky said quietly. "The forty-five percent you usually split with Dice is just on the suckers you two bring in. This five percent is on the entire take in Hart City."

My gullet relaxed suddenly and the whiskey I'd started to sip flooded a scalding path down my throat. Five percent of the mob's take! Why, if the take came to half that of Miami ...!

Silky's smile widened. He said, "Half a million, like we took this year, would net you twenty-five G's. And I don't see why we shouldn't do even better with an airtight fix. Well, what do you say?"

"What's the game?"

He handed me a heavy manila envelope and I opened it. It was filled with clippings and typewritten notes. You had to say this for Silky. When he mapped the layout for a job, he really dug out the facts.

"There's a catch," he said. He took a photograph out of his pocket and handed it to me. "The city manager's daughter. She's redheaded."

I got a real lift out of the picture. I hadn't expected anything like this. She was a slick raggle all right, lots of class. "I'm not superstitious," I said. "Remember the redhead in St. Louis? She brought us plenty of luck."

He told me her name was Deborah Owens before she was married. Now it was Deborah Clark. Her husband, Jim Clark, went overseas with the infantry, after three years was killed on Okinawa. He said, "This is mostly junk we dug up on him."

I got the angle. "You mean I was a friend of his?"

"That's right. An overseas pal. You're a cinch to get in with her fast."

I didn't like this. I said, "I'd be in a sweet spot trying to pass as an authority on the army."

Silky said sharply, "I'm not paying you five percent purely for your beauty. You'll find the essential dope in there. I'll trust you to cover for the rest. I think you're a pretty good cover-up."

A sneer was rising to the surface of his voice, and I didn't pursue the argument further. He went on giving me directions. Dice and I were to drive across country in my Cadillac. He'd follow by plane when he got things in order here. He gave me three century notes.

I said, "I can take Dice's to him."

He went on putting his wallet back into his trousers.

"That's expense money for both of you. This isn't a pleasure trip. I want you to make time. That will cover car expense and hotel rooms. You don't need suites. There's no one between here and Hart City you need to impress."

I knew that five percent was griping him. So I didn't quibble over this typical penny pinching.

"When you get to Hart City, drop Dice at the Cortez Hotel, put your car in storage, then go and get yourself a room at the Y.M.C.A."

For a minute I thought I hadn't heard him right.

He began to chortle. "That's a good one," he said. "You—the Featherbed Kid—living at the Y.M.C.A.!" He went on ribbing me, saying how good it would be for my soul, associating with those fine boys, learning about morals and my duty to humanity. When he saw he'd pushed me as far as I'd go peaceable, he told me there was a solid reason for my staying there. I'd find it when I read the dope on the husband of Deborah Clark.

"You're the boss," I said. I tried to keep it friendly.

He took me to the door, his hand on my arm. He said, "Don't mind a little joke, Rick. I'm putting you there because it's a hell of a smart move. You know that. I wouldn't be trying to ride you. I've got too much at stake on this fix. You do this job the way I know you can do it and we'll be set for keeps in this town. We'll rip and tear." He took a pin out of his pocket and attached it to my lapel. It was the kind all the veterans are wearing.

He said. "How's that for favors? I keep you out of the draft. And now I get you an honorable discharge pin."

I had to grin. I said, "Not bad."

When I got back to the apartment, Dice wasn't alone. Tory was there. She swung anklet-strapped feet down from the arm of her chair and stood up. Her red-plastered lips stayed in a pout, her blue-green eyes were narrowed. She said, "Hi ya, Baby."

I shut the door fast and tried to think if I'd noticed a possible tail as I came in. I was burned. "Why did you go to all the precaution of coming up to my room?" I asked her. "Why didn't you just meet me down on the street?"

She rose and doubled on the sarcasm. "Always thinking of that pretty skin of yours, aren't you?"

Dice was shuffling a deck of cards. He said, "Silky had Max tailing her. She shook him."

"She hopes," I said.

Tory's eyes flashed but she didn't say anything. She went over to the phone, swinging those rounded hips of hers under her tight skirt, and called a number.

She said into the phone, "Mickey? Is the big ape sleeping under his hat still in the lobby?" She pushed the receiver into

my ear then so I heard the desk boy at her apartment answer.
"Yes he is, Miss Pizarro."

"Okay," I said.

She dropped the receiver on its cradle and smiled at me. "You can stop trembling." She started her arms toward my neck, but halfway up hit me in the stomach. I went down backward against a chair. "I'm asking the questions," she said.

Dice sighed. "Watch yourself," he muttered. "She's on a rampage."

I could see this was true. There was something primitive about Tory when she was upset. Her whole body seemed to be charged with the current of her temper. It crackled out of her eyes. Her inky-black hair swung thick about her shoulders when she tossed her head.

"Silky's sending me to Havana. What's the play?"

"How do I know?"

"You know if the mob's blowing town. That's when he always sends me away. You aren't heading for Havana, are you?"

I shrugged. Better act like I was giving in. "We're blowing," I said. "I don't know where yet."

"You're a liar."

I slid down into the chair, reached over to the dresser for the bottle of whiskey and poured myself a drink. "Why don't you ask Silky?" I suggested.

She came over as I drank. She lifted up her spike heel and brought it down with all her force on my foot. "I'm asking you."

Crushing pains shot through my toes but I finished my drink. Then I put down the glass, grabbed her arm and yanked her onto my lap. I said, "Silky's still the inside man, baby. He's running the mob. When I'm running it, maybe I'll tell you."

She lay back against me breathing hard. She said, "Maybe I won't wait till you're running the mob."

"You'll wait."

She pushed back from me all of a sudden and ran her hand inside my coat. I realized too late she'd been lying against the stiff photo of Deborah Clark.

"What's this?" She yanked it back when I reached for it and opened it. I could feel her breath stop, her body tense.

"Who is it?"

"It's my kid sister."

She gave it another look. "If that's your kid sister, I'm a snake's belly."

I said, "Well?"

She tried to tear the picture, but I got it away from her and kicked it toward the table. She grabbed a handful of my hair and, when I broke her hold, bit me. She was calling me every name she could lay her tongue to, which was plenty.

I saw Dice pick up the picture, look at it and toss it into my bureau drawer. She was writhing and trying to scratch me now. I pinned her arms to her sides.

She spat at me. She jeered, "Yaaaa! Want to keep pretty for the doll!"

"That's right."

"I'll make you pretty, you damned conceited phony!" A boa constrictor with heels, that was Tory when she was mad. I was gasping myself.

"Lay off, you hyena!" I yelled at her. "I get it. You're jealous. You're crazy about me. What else are you trying for?"

She let out a low scream of raw fury and threw herself against me to trip me back over a stool. Her body was hot, pulsing with fury. I began to laugh as I fought her. Dice picked up his hat and went away, slamming the door. I knew he'd stay away for a couple of hours.

## Chapter 3

The Cadillac was singing along like a choirboy. A sign said ten more miles to Hart City. Dice was crumpled over in the seat pounding his ear. He hadn't said ten words since we left El Paso. His stomach ulcers had been giving him hell. Fish, he said it was, that had stayed away from home too long.

I took one hand off the wheel long enough to shake him awake. He looked at me like murder would have been too good.

"What's the idea?" he snarled.

"We're almost there. Thought I'd give you time to fix your lipstick."

For answer I got a sour look. He straightened in the seat, adjusted his necktie, smoothed his hair with his hands and fished his grey hat from back of the seat.

He shivered. "Colder than hell."

"This isn't Florida," I reminded him.

To our right a range of moss-green mountains leaned against the china-blue sky. The Coastal Highway skirted the Pacific with only a yellow ribbon of beach separating the concrete slab from the sea. The air was cold and tangy with the smell of salt mixed with sage and eucalyptus.

Dice whistled sharply. "Not bad!"

We were passing a plushy joint that spread over an acre or so with lawns running down to the ocean. The sign over the entrance said, "Vista Del Mar."

"Yeah, I know about that," Dice griped. "Twenty slugs a day. Silky's parking there. But you and me we gotta hold expenses down to ten a day."

I knew he was burned so I didn't say any more about it. Me, I was feeling higher than the Empire State. These four days of driving had been a tonic. Nine hours' sleep every night and no fear of being sneezed. I started humming to myself. The world right now seemed about the size of a tennis ball, and I was toying with it in the palm of my hand. A flock of gulls minced coyly along the sand and then went screaming overhead.

Out of the corner of my eye I could see Dice was taking in the lay of the land.

"I'll have smallpox for a while," I said. "It wouldn't be good for us to be seen together."

"I don't love you that much, sweetheart. A rest from that ugly pan of yours will do me good."

I looked at him hard. "And for chrissake stay out of trouble. No subway dealing to these yokels or you might get us all in stir."

Dice turned to me with a humorless smile. "I brought my crocheting, Grandma. I'm doing a pot cover in the poison ivy design. And for you."

I laughed. That Dice was a card.

The highway widened to four lanes. We were getting almost into the town. It sure was different from Florida. The languor was gone. The gentleness of the breeze. Here the air was snappy and brittle. Made a man feel vitality running riot through his veins.

We breezed under a plastered arch that had *Welcome* in six-foot letters. I cut the speed down to thirty-five. Houses, mostly white stucco, sat symmetrically on squares of bright green lawns. Kids shot each other noisily with toy guns along the parkway while amateur Burbanks pruned rosebushes or pushed lawn mowers with a high whirring sound.

As we started through the tangle of traffic in the business section, Dice said, "This boiler's pretty conspicuous in a small town. And the 1946 Florida tags won't look too good for a guy who's spent two years in the South Pacific."

"I'm putting it in storage," I told him. "I can rent a U-Drive-It to get around in."

I noticed a sign up the street advertising cars for rent by the week or month.

We slid up to the curbing in front of the Cortez. It was a white stucco building with deep-set gothic windows and brightly painted ornamental iron grills. Red tiles paved the steps and lobby entrance. It didn't look too bad.

Dice was sliding his bag off the back seat.

"Not much like the Surfton, eh?" I cracked.

His face broke into a smile. "Still better than a berth at the Y."

For a minute he forgot his ulcers. He threw his head back and laughed like hell. When he stopped there were tears in his eyes. "Jesus! that strikes me funny. The Featherbed Kid putting up at the Y.M.C.A.!"

I cruised up the main street to the storage garage. A punk kid came out of the office tearing a stub from a parking ticket.

"Overnight?" he asked.

I climbed out and stretched my legs. I was stiff from sitting. "Put it in moth balls. I won't be needing it again for a couple of weeks."

The punk's eyebrows went up. "Dead storage, sir?"

"Not too dead. See that the battery doesn't run down and watch it for flats."

I slipped a couple of singles from my trousers pocket and shoved them into the kid's hand. "This is for you, sonny. I'll take care of the storage when I check out."

He grinned and thanked me as he folded the bills into the pocket of his khaki shirt.

While I unlocked the turtleback to get my Gladstone, the kid stood watching me. After I'd locked it up again, I tossed him the keys. "Another thing," I said. "Keep those keys in the cash register in the office. Don't give them to anyone but me. Not even if the guy tells you he's my long-lost pappy. If he tries to butter your palm, I'll double it. Same goes for the night man."

I was thinking of the time in Chicago when I first bought the car. Dice got a notion at two in the morning to run some raggle up to Milwaukee for a glass of beer. The streets were icy and they slid into a telephone pole in Evanston and cracked an axle. We couldn't have any hitches on this job if we had to make a run for it.

It was two blocks to the U-Drive-It place. A small chubby woman with black beads for eyes smiled happily at me while I counted out seventy bucks for two weeks in advance. She nodded toward a Pontiac sedan in the lot and gave me the keys while I folded my receipt. I drove to the Y.M.C.A. and parked around in back. There was a half-filled lot with no attendant in charge.

The building was five stories, light-grey limestone, and looked like a bank. As I crossed the terra-cotta floor of the lobby I got a glimpse of a short, fat man, sitting behind the desk. He grinned up at me apologetically after a minute and stopped burrowing through the mass of papers on his desk.

"Mislaid my watch again," he explained. He beamed at me vaguely. "They tell me I'm absent-minded."

I pointed the watch out over by the inkwell.

He grabbed it with a rueful and relieved snort. "I do declare. Right under my eyes." He thanked me profusely and slipped the watch into his vest pocket. "Ought to keep it in a safe-deposit vault, I guess. Family heirloom. Couple of real diamonds in it."

"Might be safer," I agreed.

He put out his hand. I didn't mean to wring it so hard, but I saw him wince.

"Welcome to Hart City. You're a stranger in town, aren't you?"

"Yes. First stop here."

"I'm Charley Meyer. Secretary of the Y."

I said, "I'd like a single room for a couple of days, Mr. Meyer."

His head cocked over to the side. "No mister stuff here," he cried. "I'm Charley. Just plain Charley to all my boys."

I stifled a laugh. The same old eyewash. The palsy-walsy stuff. But what the hell. For five percent of the take in Hart City, I'd be a kangaroo.

"In that case, the name is Rick." I used the name Silky had given me for this job. "Rick Fagan, sir."

Charley wagged his head. "The 'sir' business is out with us too." He smiled benevolently. "We're just like a family here, you know."

I grinned. "It's the army training. Three years as an enlisted man." I'd given up this dope's seeing my discharge button by himself.

His smile brightened. "In that case, you're excused. And I might add, doubly welcome. Anyone who has served his country is just about right with me."

It was the opening I'd been angling for. I decided to toss in my hat. "Friend of Jim Clark's," I said quietly.

"Jim Clark!"

He stared at me and the smirk of welcome on his fat face disappeared as if I'd slapped him. Moisture formed behind his polished glasses. He jerked them off and began to wipe them with his handkerchief. His voice was choked up. He said, "Jim was one of my boys."

"I know."

He hitched his glasses up over his ears again, sighing. "We lost a lot of boys in this town," he said. "Fine lads, all of them. But Jim was just one of those rare souls everyone loved. Worthwhile, fine ideals, still a man's man."

I lowered my voice to match his. "Yeah. Jim was a great guy."

It was like sitting in the stock exchange and seeing a stock you had heavy sugar on skyrocket twenty points. Anyone who was a friend of this Jim Clark's evidently was a bit of all right in Hart City. Silky had the right dope. No doubt of that.

Charley was getting his composure back. "Know his wife?" he asked.

"Not yet. That's why I stopped off here, on my way East."

He gave me a speculative little smile. "I'll bet Jim asked you to stop. I know how he was. Always thinking of Deborah—how she'd take it if anything happened."

"That's right." I made the words stick in my throat.

I thought he was going to blubber. This guy could have made a fortune in *East Lynne*. He leaned across the desk and lowered his voice further. "Deborah Clark's a wonderful girl," he said. "One of the best."

"Jim thought so," I murmured.

"But this ordeal has been mighty hard on her."

There was a look in his eye I didn't like. "What do you mean?" I asked.

"She's been in a sanitarium, you know. Went completely to pieces."

"No!" I didn't have to shove in the concern on this one. This was the end of a million-dollar dream. "How long will she be there?"

"Oh she's out. Been home over a month. But she still isn't so good. Won't see any of her old friends. Just stays to herself."

I could have socked the old geezer for giving me a jolt like this. Then my anger turned back on Silky. Damn him, why didn't he tell me this? A hundred to one the dame wouldn't see me.

"Maybe I've stopped for nothing," I said.

Charley looked sympathetic. "She might see you on account of your being a buddy of Jim's," he said doubtfully, "but—well, you know how it is."

"Sure ... sure ..." I said. I wasn't kidding. I knew how it was, all right. If I blew this job, I'd probably be back riding trains, playing the short con for coffee and cakes. I felt low all at once.

I signed the register then and he handed me a key.

"Rick ... maybe I shouldn't ask you this...."

He was grinning at me apologetically as if I'd known the favor he was trying to ask. I smiled back. It was all he needed.

"Tonight is our monthly boys' meeting. Jim was a Junior leader, you know. The best one we ever had. The boys worshipped him. I wondered if it would he too much to ask, you being a friend of Jim's and all, if you'd say a few words to them."

Christ! You could have flattened me with a feather! I've done a lot of screwy things in my time, but here was really one for the book. I had to play it straight.

"Well," I said, feeling my way along, "I'd like to do it for you, Charley, but I'm afraid I'm like most soldiers when it comes to talking about their war experiences. There's so much bitterness and sorrow tied up with it. It's one of those things you try to forget."

He picked a piece of lint off my sleeve. I could tell by the look in those cherubic blue eyes of his he wasn't taking this for an answer.

"I didn't mean war necessarily," he said. "Not that they wouldn't enjoy it—you know how boys are. But they'd like to hear anything you wanted to talk about. I thought some general topic—anything you'd like." His pudgy fingers pulled nervously at the points of his vest. You'd have thought his job depended on this speech of mine.

I had an idea. I grinned. "Something like 'the value of honesty'?"

His beam returned. "Splendid! Simply splendid."

I slapped him on the back. "All right, Charley," I promised. "I'll work something up. Ten minutes be enough?"

He said ten minutes would be fine. Or as long as I wanted. "We'll expect you at seven then. We eat first and then have the talks."

Suitcases in hand, I was almost to the elevator when Charley puffed up again.

"There's one more thing," he panted. "Our organization always welcomes good publicity. Especially with the Community Chest drive only a month away. Contributions help keep our doors open, you know. A reporter from the *Gazette* would be glad to drop around and take down what you say. Any objections? I always make it a practice to ask."

That would be just swell smearing my name all over page one. Having all the mothers of servicemen dropping around to ask me questions I couldn't answer. Still I knew I had to play it smart.

"As far as I'm concerned, I wouldn't mind," I said. I laid my hand on Charley's arm and squeezed. I spoke low.

"I'm thinking about his wife though. Pretty tough on her, don't you think? People asking questions. The telephone ringing itself off the wall."

Charley came up for the bait. "You're right at that," he agreed. "It wouldn't be fair to her."

On the way up in the elevator I was thinking what a really smooth operator I was. Charley was so sold on me it was pathetic. This was going to be child's play if he was a sample of the people in Hart City.

I let myself into my room with the key he had given me. It was clean but drab. Tan walls, shining with a fresh coat of paint, a single iron bed, dresser and lowboy to match. The floor had a chocolate-brown carpet that looked almost new. On the wall there was a telephone. I slipped something out of my side coat pocket and stood looking at it nestled in the palm of my hand. It was Charley Meyer's gold watch. He hadn't noticed when I dipped it. Right there while I was talking to him. Jesus, and they call guys like that smart! I had plans for that watch.

I fished around in my Gladstone and found the heavy brown

envelope with the newspaper clippings Silky had given me—everything that had been printed about this Clark dame, her husband and her father, City Manager Owens. I scanned them again for the last time to make sure I had all the facts. Then I went to the phone and dialed her number.

It rang quite a while before anyone answered. I was beginning to get jittery when the thin, impersonal voice of a maid said, "Owens residence."

I asked to speak to Mrs. Clark.

"Couldn't I take the message?"

"Sure. Don't disturb her," I said, not letting any sarcasm leak through. "I was with her husband on Okinawa. Just passing through town. He asked me to stop and pay my respects."

There was silence. I hoped it was a startled one. But all she said was, "I'll give her the message."

"Fagan's the name. I'm down at the Y.M.C.A." I hung up.

Hell of a reception I was getting. The filly wouldn't even talk to me on the telephone. Silently I cursed Silky and his brainstorm. Living in a dump like this Y, hobnobbing with a chump like Charley—and now a neurotic for a mark! Some setup!

There might be a silver lining though. Maybe he was still in Miami. I could get him on the phone tonight and sell him on forgetting this Hart City nightmare and meeting him in St. Paul.

I unpacked a fifth of bourbon, got a water glass from the bathroom and drank a toast to a wall sign that read, "No drinking of intoxicating beverages in this room."

I'd just finished a hot shower when the phone rang. It was a girl's voice. "Mr. Fagan?"

"Yes."

"This is Deborah Clark."

I've always said dames would steer clear of telephones if they could hear what wires do to their voices. The low ones come through harsh and the high ones squeaky. But this Clark kitten was the exception. It packed voltage, that voice of hers. Quiet, low, rich. Mr. Bell's wires hadn't touched it. She could have been in my arms.

"Hello!"

I jolted out of my dreaming. Told her it was nice of her to call me back.

She said, "I got your message. I'm waiting down in the lobby. Can you come to the house for tea?"

There was no fooling around about this raggle. I liked her better by the second. And if this was the voice of a neurotic, I was a hunchbacked moron! Standing there, stripped, watching the water trickle down on Charley's new carpet, I began to feel a new glow. I let the glow melt into my words.

"I'd like nothing better. I'll be down in five minutes."

Exactly three minutes later I surveyed myself in the mirror. A conservative brown tweed suit, maroon knitted tie, brown and white sport oxfords. I gave my hair a final brush. "Fagan," I said "for a woman with shot nerves, you're exactly what the doctor should order!"

I walked down the stairs. It made a better entrance than sidling out of the creaky elevator. And a guy back from overseas would be itching for the exercise.

She was standing by the desk talking to Charley. I couldn't have missed her in a dark room. She had a mop of hair that looked like somebody had touched a match to, creamy skin, and features strictly patrician.

Her suit was loose tweeds and looked like she'd shrugged into it. But somehow it didn't hurt that slim figure of hers any more than telephone wires had hurt the timbre of her voice.

Charley saw me first, and his sunshine and benevolent smile almost hit his ears. She turned then. Her eyebrows went up slightly. Her eyes were azure blue.

Charley said, "This is our boy right now." Pride and fellowship oozed out of his voice.

The Clark dame held out her hand. "This was so nice of you, Mr. Fagan."

"The pleasure is mine." I made it warm, but not too warm. I let go her hand after the prescribed extra minute for a special friend. I could tell now how nervous she was. That soft little mitt of hers gave it away. It was cold as ice and it had a tremor in it.

"My car's outside."

It was a blue Buick coupé, a nice conservative job that the young matron Clark would own. She drove faster than the law allowed. Once a cop pulled up beside us on a motorcycle and I thought, "Here's a ticket for you, sister." But he only touched his finger to his cap, grinned at her, and went on by.

Not so bad being the city manager's kid!

There were some pretty nice houses on the road she took toward the hills. But when she stopped, it was before an old stucco affair that looked meek and careworn.

It was cool inside. There was so much furniture, I stumbled over a couple of chairs trying to get to the one she pointed out.

"It's a little cluttered, I'm afraid," she said. "I brought my furniture with me when I moved back in with Father." She passed a slender hand over her forehead and looked around the room as if she hadn't noticed it for a long time. "I suppose I should have sold my furniture."

I settled back comfortably and gave her a grin. "Well, don't sell this," I said, "I like it."

She looked at me, puzzling out my words. Then she smiled back at me a little vaguely. She said, "I'm glad."

A woman came to the door. She had on a gingham dress, but a professional look in her eye. I guessed she was a nurse-companion. She said briskly, "Well, you're back quick, Mrs. Clark."

Deborah introduced me to her. The woman asked if we wouldn't like some tea.

"I made some scones," she said temptingly.

Deborah said yes, that would be nice. She looked at me. "If you'd like it?"

I said I loved scones.

She sat facing me, her back straight, a hostess smile on her lips. The shock of hearing of me, of meeting me had worn off. She was retreating into her shell. Deadness was greying the azure blue of her eyes. I had to move fast or I'd have a dull séance ahead of me.

I leaned forward a little. I said, "Stop me if I get out of line. Being out where I was may have made too much of a barbarian out of me. But—well, I'm used to calling my friends Joe or Pete or Bill. This Mr. and Mrs. stuff is kind of hard to get back to."

She frowned. "You mean you don't want to call me Mrs. Clark?"

"Oh, I will," I said hastily. "Only, if you had any other little moniker lying around handy...."

It was the nurse who saved me. Coming in with the tea tray, she laughed with false heartiness, humoring her patient. "Well, seeing he's Jim's friend," she said, "I don't see why he shouldn't call you Deborah."

I carried on the heartiness. "Make it Deb," I said. "I'm Rick." I leaned forward and shook her hand. The color deepened in her cheeks again.

She said, "Tell me about Jim. Tell me everything you know about him."

The nurse was pouring the tea. Over Deb's shoulder she gave me a violent nod. I gathered that I was on the doctor's orders list. Some of this new psychiatric treatment probably. Making patients face things. Keeping them from escapism. It was a break for me, all right.

The nurse passed us sugar and cream, and left. I stirred my tea thoughtfully. I didn't want to go yipping on about Jim till she tripped me up. My plan was to dish it out just a little stronger than she could take it, and that way force the talk around to safer topics.

I lowered my voice. I said, "I know that you were the last person he thought of."

Her hands tightened on the chair arms. Her eyes stayed on my face.

She whispered. "Did he ...? That is, he didn't happen to ...?"

"Send you a message?"

She nodded.

"Yes. He did."

The color drained out of that pretty face of hers. She sat there looking at me and holding her breath. And all at once I hated to have to go on lying to her. Damn Silky!

But what else could I do? I couldn't stop there and tell her to forget it, that I'd never seen this Jim of hers. I went into the tale as we'd fixed it up from the newspaper accounts of Jim's heroism.

I started it with Jim and me on the boat trying to eat breakfast, hours before dawn, with our stomachs cold, tied in knots. I got us on the LST side by side headed through the breakers for the coral.

"That's when he gave me the message," I said. "He had a funny smile on his face, kind of quiet, as if he was listening to something besides the barrage the big boats behind us were putting up. He said, 'Rick, you know how I feel about her. I've bored you with it enough. If you get through, will you stop by and tell her?'"

She drew one quivering breath, just enough to ask, "And then?"

I saw she wouldn't be satisfied till she'd heard the end. I went into the murderous charge of the first assault wave. I told her of the bullet that had Jim's name on it. The room was so still my low voice seemed like a shout as I worked into the curtain lines. "I had his head in my arms ... he smiled at me, that swell grin of his ... he had a hard time getting it out but he did it ... two words. He said, *Tell her....*'"

I put my hand over hers. I said, "I guess I don't have to tell you how he felt about you. You know, don't you?"

Those eyes of hers were azure pools but she wasn't crying. She sat there looking at me, just looking at me and not seeing me. It gave me the creeps. After a couple of ages she seemed to focus again. She gave me what might pass in colder climates for a smile and said something so low I almost missed it.

"Thank you—Rick."

Then all at once she was on her feet and running out of the room.

I waited. I began to get uneasy. I wondered if I'd made it too strong. Sending her back to the sanitarium would be a hell of a way to start off the play!

But after a while she came back. She picked up her teacup and began to talk as if she hadn't been gone.

"Tell me about yourself."

So she didn't want to hear any more about Jim. Well, my little game had paid off anyway. I began giving her the tale Silky and I had built up about my boyhood.

"I was raised—excuse me, I mean *reared*, by an Aunt Phoebe in Philadelphia," I told her. "Germantown. Her aim in life was to make me a child out of this world. She nearly succeeded." I related harrowing experiences of me—a Lord Fauntleroy joker—thrown into boarding schools.

This was a hot one. I'd been in Philly then all right—but with the circus as one of its youngest grifters.

I went on to her about a day I entered Lawrenceville in the second form in a Buster Brown collar and Eton jacket, and the reception I got from the other students.

She finally cracked through to the fact that it was funny. Her laugh was strictly *ersatz* but I thought the nurse, coming in to pass scones, was going to kiss me.

I went on from there to my Princeton days. I wasn't worried about being caught up on any details here. I'd spent a couple of years on some of the better campuses wearing a variety of fraternity pins and selling various histories of the house (which never turned up) in morocco for ten bucks a shot to my brothers.

I could tell by the look on her pan she was trying to keep her mind on me so it wouldn't go back to Jim right now.

"And when you finished school?"

This I could answer straight. "Oh, traveled a lot, worked now and then."

Which brought us up to the war. For fear she hadn't taken enough punishment, I looked at my watch. I showed polite surprise. "It's after five!"

"Is it?" She sounded relieved. "Why, the afternoon hasn't been long at all."

She took me to the door before she could figure out what it was she wanted. Then she popped out with an invitation to dinner.

"I'd like you to meet my father."

"I'd like to meet him," I said. And this was on the level too. But I knew I couldn't. My next move was the hard-to-get. Disappear and let her think me over. Luckily I had a solid excuse. I told her of my promise to speak to the junior boys at the Y.

"Oh."

She was a little confused at being disappointed over something again. She said, "How long can you stay in town?"

I said, "I ought to shove along tomorrow. My aunt's quite upset over my stopping off at all."

"Of course." She seemed to accept it. She smiled at me politely and held out her hand. "It was very nice of you to come. Thank you. Good-bye."

The door shut before I was down to the second step. Firm and quick. Well, how do you like that!

The nurse was waiting in the car to drive me back. She thanked me too. She said I'd had a good influence on Deb.

I began to feel better. After all, I couldn't expect a high-strung, nervous filly like this one to hang on my neck the first night. I'd probably made as much progress as was possible under the circumstances. And she still had life in her. Too much to let that aunt routine stop her. She'd think of some way to keep me. Of course if she didn't, I could always fall back on the can't-get-reservations gag.

## Chapter 4

Over the steam table of the Y cafeteria was a motto, reading: "Make your first rule for success the Golden Rule. *And as ye would that men should do to you, do ye also to them likewise.*"

I got a big cheer out of it. It took me back to my circus days when I'd taken a shine to a sucker kid in Philly, Pete Martin, who'd got the job of watering the elephants for his admission. I sneaked out one Sunday and went to Sunday school with him. When I got home all aquiver with the music and the colored leaflet and big talk about this Golden Rule, my father howled with laughter.

"The greatest grifter of all days was the guy who thought up this Golden Rule," he told me. "He put a good hunk of the world on the sucker lists. And while these addicts are running around thinking of their fellow man, the smart guy can step in and clean up."

Strictly a small-timer, my father never had the stuff to get beyond three-card monte and faro with a tell box, but he had the fundamentals.

Charley was shoving his battered aluminum tray along behind mine. "You like the plaque?" he beamed.

"You couldn't have a better one," I said wholeheartedly.

"Fill up his plate, boys, pile it up," he called to the boys behind the counter. "Good plain food and plenty of it. That's what we give here at the Y."

They took him at his word. I had to stop them. "Just a minute, fellas! I've got a good appetite but I'm not a Newfoundland!"

It went on like this after we got to the table. Charley calling over boys and starting to blow about me. I sticking a modest barb into his balloon, and the boys joining in Charley's hearty guffaws.

I knew it was a publicity campaign for my talk tonight, and it got pretty dull.

More and more I was convinced this Y.M.C.A. stuff was unnecessary color, and Silky was probably using it just to annoy me. Maybe to make sure I wouldn't be boarding Tory.

The "good plain food" sank with dull thuds into my cold stomach. I wished to hell I hadn't been so chicken about that bottle of whiskey in my room before dinner. Of all nights to go without a slug!

I decided I'd angle out of that talk anyway. That was one half-hour of boredom I could do without. A telegram? A long-distance call? I was working on the best angle as Charley guided me from the dining room. He waved the boys to come right along. So it would have to be a forgotten long-distance call I must put in at the station down the street.

But the minute we entered the meeting room, I knew I'd have to speak. Deb Clark was sitting on the back row of chairs! Luckily the kids swarmed in past us, in such a pell-mell surge there was no chance to go back and greet her. I gave her a wave, and she waved back, then huddled down in her chair and pulled her coat collar up around her neck so the boys wouldn't notice her.

Behind my smile I was churning pretty desperately. What the devil was I going to say!

Charley pushed me up onto a raised dais and clapped his hands to quiet the yelling and chair scraping.

"Boys," he said, "I guess I don't have to introduce this man to you."

Cheers and whistles answered him. Old Charley should have been a press agent. I could see by the excitement and hero worship in their eyes how full he'd pumped them of my supposed Okinawa exploits. It gave me my opening.

I made it flat. I said, "Boys, I'm not going to talk about the war."

And watched the little devils deflate.

Then I said, "Sure, I was at Okinawa. Under the hell of the opening barrage from the battle babies, wading into shore with a heavy pack and a gun to keep dry, diving for shell holes after each bad explosion to keep clear of shrapnel, charging an enemy gun emplacement at night with the sky like a Fourth of July fireworks and tracers passing so close you could smell the smoke...."

They were with me again to the last man. Breathless, sitting forward, hanging onto my words. And the enthusiasm of a bunch of teenage boys is intoxicating. I was almost caught by it. Stories I'd read of the battle flooded back. I started stringing them along and they loved it.

And then I happened to get a look at Deb Clark. The lines around her mouth told me she couldn't take much more of this.

I switched but fast.

I told them all this action we'd seen was just a prelude to the battles ahead. "This is the front lines now, fellas," I said, "and there'll be plenty of barrages, shrapnel, gun emplacements, shell holes. There'll be fear and glory, Purple Hearts and traitors."

Then I remembered the theme I'd promised Charley. And I worked into it really fancy. My voice swelled out like that evangelist I'd heard at Winona Lake, the one whose treasurer we took for twenty-five grand. I said, "You've been drafted into the greatest battle—maybe the last battle of civilization! This isn't penny ante anymore. This isn't any scrap over territory. Or vague ideologies. This is it. The showdown. The battle to see if human beings can live on this earth together, or if they must annihilate themselves.

"There are only two armies now. The army fighting for peace, and the army fighting for destruction. Which are you for?"

A frenzied battle cry answered me. "Peace! Yay! Peace!" These little hoodlums had plenty of guts.

"It won't be any easy battle," I outshouted them. "The enemy is tricky. He will try infiltration in a hundred disguises. You will have to face him on a thousand fronts. You must be constantly on the alert, and armed. Armed with the one weapon he can't prevail against—honesty! Honesty with yourselves, honesty with each other!"

I took a deep breath while this sank in. The silence was sharp. I said slowly, "That's what we ask of you, we coming back from this last war. Alertness, honesty, a determined demand for peace. Are you willing to take up the battle?"

The wild salvo of cheers, stamps, whistles almost blew the ceiling off the room.

Charley leaped to his feet, motioned for silence and offered belligerent prayer, thanking God for warriors like me.

Christ, I hoped the Almighty had a sense of humor.

I mopped my forehead and found I needed it. I'd really been in there pitching! The waves of violent enthusiasm bouncing around that room had me walking on bubbles.

Deb Clark was wiping her eyes when I finally got to her through that swarm of young hoodlums. I said, "I'm afraid I bored you stiff."

She shook her head hard. "Oh, no! I hope you didn't mind my dropping in."

Does a fisherman mind if the twenty-pounder leaps for the hook? I risked a discreet squeeze of her hand. I said, "What do you think?"

She smiled at me and she didn't pull away her hand. "Would you like to go for a little ride—or maybe you have something more important to do." This was an understatement.

I went up for my coat. As I'd figured, Charley was still talking to Deb in the lobby when I came down again. I hauled his gold watch from my pocket and gave it to him.

"Isn't this yours?"

Charley practically scooped out his tonsils in his gulp.

"Funny thing happened," I said. "A kid came up to me in the hall upstairs and asked if I'd give it back to you." I looked puzzled. "One of the kids who'd been in there just now listening to me blab."

Charley sucked in his breath. Then he began to shake his head and cluck. "Well, what do you know about that," he said. "I missed it late this afternoon." He put his hand on my shoulder. "I knew that talk would strike home, Rick." His voice quavered.

Deb Clark had it now. Her eyes began to shine. "You mean a boy had taken it—and gave it back tonight!"

Charley nodded furiously, choked up.

I could have kissed myself. Talk about convincers!

We drove through the business district first, Deb pointing out the larger buildings in the town. She turned off up a road that wound to the top of one of the hills overlooking the ocean. She parked at the edge of a promontory and switched off the lights.

Then she sat there looking out over the sea like she'd forgotten me. I had a hunch to keep my trap shut.

When she finally opened up, I was plenty glad I did.

"This is the place Jim and I used to come," she said in a soft voice. "I've been thinking about him."

"That's funny," I said. "So have I."

"Before today," she went on like she hadn't heard me, "I haven't let myself think of him. I was afraid to. I was afraid if I thought about it, I'd know he was dead. And I—I couldn't bear it.

"I didn't want to leave the sanitarium, but the doctor said I had to. When you called today, the nurse said I should see you. After you left, I drove and drove. I thought I couldn't stand it. I came up here. I—started to release the brake. It would have been so easy, but I thought of Dad and I couldn't do it...." She was trembling.

I was shivering a little myself. Driving marks to suicide would be a swell rep to get hung with! I'd have to watch my step closer with this jittery Jill.

"Then tonight when you were talking," she was whispering low, "all at once I began to feel better. You were saying all the things Jim would have said if he'd come back. It kind of seemed as if what Jim believed in, what he was working for, was going right on. And somehow, he was going on in it ..."

She was trembling harder now but her eyes were shining as the words tumbled out of her. All about this joker, Jim. How, while he was on the All-American football team in college he'd given some talks to problem-group boys for the Probation Department, and had moved on into boys' work for the city.

How he'd had a lot of bugs in his bonnet about most bad boys being only bored boys, and it was the city's responsibility to provide for its boys' spare hours. He'd inaugurated some dopey system of colored pins on maps showing areas where truancy and general juvenile delinquency were on the increase. He'd send boys out there to lie around vacant lots with baseball bats and mitts, who'd infiltrate into gangs and direct their activity, without the poor kids knowing they were being directed.

What a racket!

She rattled off statistics like an almanac. "Federal Bureau of Investigation reports for 1940 showed that 12 percent of all murderers, 45 percent of all burglars, 32 percent of all thieves, 15 percent of all arsonists, and 52 percent of all automobile thieves apprehended were under the age of 21."

"That's terrific," I said. I meant it. I was thinking with a memory like that what a help she could be to a man in my profession.

"Statistics indicate," she said, "that 75 percent of adult criminals have graduated into that state from juvenile delinquency. You can see why Jim felt, as you do, that the destiny of the world depends upon the stature of its youth."

Youth ... While I gave her her head, my mind went back to the circus game my father worked out for me when I was just about able to walk. In a sloppy pair of pants cut down from his, I'd stand in the crowd at the big gate till I spotted a prosperous sucker, then I'd yell my lungs out about being lost, grab his hand and lead him back to my father, who'd be so grateful to him he'd let him in on a faro game. God, what a training I had! Not one grifter in five hundred had had my advantages.

After a while she turned those blue beacons of hers on me and asked, "Did Jim ever tell you of his plans?"

"Well, some of them."

"Of the city recreation center, where boys can always find activity, ball games, classes, model building of every kind. With directors ready to instruct and organize their interests?"

"Yeah," I said. "It was a great idea."

"He had it all worked out, you know. He was ready to start raising the money for it when he was drafted. A lot of other towns all over the country were interested in it. Once it was built, the city clubs and churches would keep it up."

All of a sudden I had a great idea myself. This ought to be good for several days' stay in Hart City anyway.

"I feel like you do, Deb," I said. "This work of Jim's has got to go on. It's what he'd want. This town thought a lot of him. I'll bet if we approached the right ones, they'd build this center as a memorial to him."

The moon had come up. It platinumed her face above the black of her coat, and highlighted that mop of gold she used for hair.

She looked at me a long time without saying anything. Then she whispered, "I knew you'd think of something. Something I could go on living for. But the city won't start it."

"If they don't, they're a bunch of cheap ..."

"I want to do it myself."

"Have you any idea how much money it would take?" I said gently.

"Yes. And I have it. Three hundred thousand. Mother's estate that Dad would never touch. She left it to me." It goes to show you're never too smart to get jolted! Three hundred Gs! Real cash! And on this little green tomato!

## Chapter 5

I went back to Dice's room at the Cortez feeling pretty good. Things were going smooth as a breeze. And I couldn't complain about the company I had for the job either. Deb Clark was a really nice girl. I liked being with her. After the dames I knew, she was restful as a pretty child with a sand pail, and as transparent. I thought of what Tory would have made of the opportunity I'd given Deb this evening. Tory would have figured a guy in the arms was worth three dead husbands in the bush. Tory was a dame who lived strictly in the present. And how!

Tonight I wished Havana weren't so far away. I wondered if I'd been too scared of this job, not letting her come along.

Dice opened the door for me. He was comfortable with a rye. He ordered me a Haig and Haig but I didn't wait. I poured myself some of his rye, though I don't go for the stuff. I went around his room enjoying the thick rug, feeling the curtains.

"All this elegance goes to a guy's head," I said.

Dice began a hacking laugh.

"I wake up hysterical," he said, "thinking of the Featherbed Kid stashed away in a boys' barracks."

I poured myself another slug of rye and eased into a chair. "Don't worry," I told him, "this isn't going to last long." I lifted my glass and made a toast.

"To the good things of life—Chinese rugs and featherbeds. Strong liquor and weak women."

Dice's face told me first. Before I heard the hard slam of the door. I swung around.

It was Silky standing there looking like he had hold of a couple of thousand volts and couldn't let go. I got up fast.

He said in that smooth monotone of his that hits you like the rasping of a rattler, "So you're the one who sent for her."

"Sent for who?"

He didn't take his eyes off me while he reached in his pocket. I went cold for a minute. But his hand came out with a yellow paper. He unfolded it and handed it to me. It was a wire from the punk he'd put on Tory's tail in Havana. It said Tory had lammed out via plane headed West.

I relaxed. I handed back the telegram. "I didn't send for her," I told him.

He kept on looking at me, trying to catch a flicker of something on my face that would tell him I was lying.

"I left her stony, on purpose," he said slowly. "*Somebody* helped her."

I said, "She'd get the money easy. But how did she know where we were?"

His eyes hardened. "Only Jerry and Max and Dice and you knew it when we started," he said. "I don't know why Jerry or Max or Dice would tell her."

I said heatedly, "Well, I don't know why you think *I* would. The kind of job I'm working on, only a fool would send for another woman, let alone a wildcat like Tory."

Silky said evenly, "You haven't been so wise in the past when it came to Tory."

I'd had about enough. I said loudly, "I thought we had that settled. She was your property and I wasn't claim jumping."

"You saw her in Miami."

"Sure. When I couldn't avoid her."

Silky went a little purple.

"Rick didn't send for her." Dice jumped in trying to smooth things over. "She's probably gone to Chicago or someplace."

"When I send for her," I said, "it'll be after you and I have split up. Or maybe you'd like that now? Maybe you'd like to forget this Hart City job? For my money, one evening at that Y.M.C.A. and that five percent doesn't seem so indispensable."

The boy came in right now with the Haig and Haig. Dice fooled around getting change for him, giving Silky time to calm down. It worked. By the time the boy had gone, Silky had relaxed. He said, "Forget it, Rick."

"Sure he will," Dice said.

"I should have known you wouldn't send for her. The goddamned little twist gets me crazy sometimes. Someday I'm going to kick her out."

"And then *I* can have her," I said to myself. "That would be

Silky's idea of generosity." But I sat down and finished my drink with him. There was no reason I should carry a grudge about it. Tory wasn't breaking up a game like this Hart City job, not if I could help it.

Silky said, "How are things going?"

"Not bad." I told him how I'd spent the afternoon and evening. I could see he was impressed with the way I'd handled Charley Meyer and the boys. And especially with the progress I'd made with Deb Clark.

I told him about the memorial gag.

"That's the stuff," Silky approved. "She'll want you to stick around and help her start it."

"It's what I'm hoping," I said.

He gave us a couple more C notes. He said, "You know how you can reach me if you want me. Don't worry about expenses."

"Sure," I said. "Just spread myself at the Y."

Silky laughed. "Better keep away from liquor. Do you think you could have her ready for the play in a couple of days?"

"I doubt it."

"How long?"

"I'm not sure yet. We're not dealing with any mud-kicker, you know. She's one of these Christ-bitten dolls, and getting her into a fraud game, even for me, is going to take doing."

"I hope it won't take more than a week."

"So do I."

After Silky had gone, I took a shot of Haig and Haig. Dice said, "Silky said to lay off."

"How can I drink to Tory without liquor?"

He was peeved. "You didn't send for her, did you?"

"No."

"Well if she does end up here, for God's sake, stay out of her way, will you?"

"Maybe I will and maybe I won't."

Dice groaned. "Here we go again."

"She may look pretty good to me after a couple more nights of that Y.M.C.A. and swapping ideals with Deb Clark," I pointed out. "Anyway, Silky doesn't own her, and I don't like the way he thinks he does."

"He's the big guy."

"Okay, okay, so he is! I still say, if he was regular he'd give up a babe that went for another grifter."

"I'm not saying he's been regular about it," Dice said. "All I'm saying is, if you want to keep on being a roper for him you better forget that dame."

I said, "Maybe I'm getting a little fed up being a roper for him. Maybe I could give the marks the play as well as he does."

"And you'd better forget that too, along with the dame."

"I'll bet," I said, "if you and I started out tomorrow and picked up a mob, we could beat Silky's time in six months."

Dice got out his cards with a sigh. "Maybe so. But it would take money. And we haven't got it. So …"

"Well, after this Hart City job …"

"Don't make me laugh," Dice said. "That five percent will come in in dribbles. You'll be borrowing from me between payoffs."

"Supposing I know where I can get three hundred Gs?" I told him about the secret cush this Clark dame had. "I could get it like that."

Up to now, I had just been shooting off my mouth. But all of a sudden the thing kind of added up. It sounded pretty good. I tried to sell it to Dice but he didn't go for it.

"You're just sore at Silky," he said. "Go home and sleep it off. We're sitting pretty and you know it."

"I don't get along with Silky."

"You always did till this Pizarro dame came along. You will again as soon as you come to your senses and give her the brush."

He had a couple of cups of coffee sent up. And he made me take a perfumed Breatheze before I left.

"My God," I said, "is this the way the other half lives?"

I went back to the Y. The place had all the life of a bear's den in the dead of winter. Even the night clerk looked doped. I went up to my room and took off my clothes and got into bed. But I didn't go to sleep right away. This idea I'd spilled to Dice kept pulling at the corners of my mind.

Everything Dice had said was true. I had to admit it. Still, if I was ever going to make the top I had to keep breaking out of even good setups. I'd read a book once on learning. I remembered it said something about how you'd make progress for a while and then you'd reach a plateau and you'd have a hell of a time getting off it and starting up the next grade.

Maybe I was on a plateau. After all, the Alabama Kid was a big inside man when he was younger than I was now. Maybe I'd had too much fun being a roper, traveling the best boats and trains, stopping at the best hotels to pick up my marks.

A guy with my brains and my personality couldn't afford to stop until he hit the top. I thought of the way I handled that crowd of boys tonight. Could Silky have done that? No. Yet he had an eighty-foot yacht and three country houses, while all I had was a few grand stashed away and a Cadillac car.

A man had to think of his future. This might be the time to make the break.

I didn't try to make my decision tonight. Things like this I've found it's better to sleep on. I just drifted off, feeling good.

## Chapter 6

The spell of the play was on me. I knew it the minute I opened my eyes. My wristwatch said eight o'clock. Thick sunshine poured like golden liquid through my windows. Birds sang a carefree song. A sharp-edged wind from the sea carried the clean smell of salt. When I say the spell was on me, that's what I mean. Maybe I'm daffy, but that's the way I get when a play is going right. All full of poetic thoughts and nice-sounding words. Don't get me wrong. I can be as rugged as the best of them, but then at times ... Oh, hell, I don't know ... But that's the way it is.

I sang in the shower. Crosby would have blushed. I dressed in a new pair of doeskin slacks I'd given fifty bucks for on Lincoln Road. They were the color of real country cream. Next I slipped into a white Harris tweed sport coat. It fitted like paint. I smiled in the mirror.

Once out in the hall I said to myself, "Fagan, don't be a chump. Good old Charley has probably set up camp in the lobby just waiting to pounce. A breakfast table talk, no doubt."

Thank God, there was a back stairway. I found it and came out into the parking lot. I skirted the building. While I was standing in front of the Y wondering where to go for breakfast an aroma floated past that I liked. Coffee and doughnuts. I saw it then. Just a hole in the wall right next to the Y.M.C.A. entrance. I went in.

Maybe it was just the way I happened to feel. Anyway all I saw when I opened the door was a blonde. A beautiful blonde with eyes the color of her light blue uniform. Her hair was piled high on her head and crowned with a fresh gardenia. She saw me about the same time I saw her. I knew the way her soft red lips broke into a faint smile that she liked what she saw.

I slid onto a stool. Two men were sitting farther down the counter drinking coffee. One of them was a copper. He glanced at me, then went on talking. Beautiful brought me a glass of water and walked down to the other guys. I saw her scribbling out checks for them. Once she glanced up and gave me the eye.

Then she came back to me. Her blue uniform had a low-cut neck. When she asked me what I wanted, I'd almost forgotten.

Finally I pulled my eyes away from her and glanced at the menu. "Coffee and two sugared," I said.

She disappeared through a swinging door and was gone a hell of a long time to sugar two sinkers. Once I caught a glimpse of her blonde head through a small oval window in the door. Then the copper and his friend started to leave. They stood up front by the cash register a minute. Beautiful came sailing out of the kitchen and took their dough. I caught on then. She was stalling so she could have me to herself.

After she brought my order she got awfully busy polishing the counter right next to me. It struck me funny. With all the counter in that place she had to polish that one spot until I thought she'd rub through the linoleum. I got busy with the coffee and doughnuts but I could feel her eye on me.

"You're new in town," she said. Her voice was as soft as the wind.

I looked up. "Got in last night."

"I can always spot a stranger," she smiled. "I can sure tell you're from the city. L. A. or Frisco?"

"Philadelphia."

She whistled. "That's in Pennsylvania, ain't it?"

"Yeah."

"I haven't been around much," she said regretfully. "Went to Bakersfield once last summer to visit my girlfriend."

She'd quit polishing and moved over in front of me. A nice-smelling perfume wafted from her. I decided she'd taken care of that when she stayed in the kitchen so long. Her make-up too looked fresher than when I came in.

I was looking straight into those lovely glimmers of hers.

"You haven't missed much," I said. "This is about as pretty a town as I've seen—and I've been everywhere."

She noticed the honorable discharge button. "Been out of the service long?"

"A week."

"What theater?"

"South Pacific."

She shook her head. "Plenty tough out there." Her eyes moved momentarily toward the ocean and back again. "Had a kid brother in it. Expect him home any day."

I finished my coffee. Said, "Yeah, it's rough. You know I used to think I wanted to live on one of those South Sea islands. Used to read a lot about Tahiti, Bali, places like that. Sounded romantic as hell. Moonlight over glassy seas, waving palm trees, beautiful women...."

She puckered her lips.

"And now you don't ...?"

"Not with all the beautiful women back here in the States." I reached out and briefly covered her hand with mine. "Take yourself, for example, you're prettier than any girl out there."

Her cheeks flushed slightly. She pulled her hand away. But her eyes were shining like a brand-new dime.

"You're not exactly repulsive yourself." She said it fast and then started polishing the counter again. The same spot. Christ, I hoped that linoleum had endurance.

Outside in the street I heard a car door slam. Automatically I glanced out the window. It was Deb Clark's blue Buick. She climbed out and headed into the Y. My first impulse was to go after her. Then I wised. A moment of disappointment is good for a dame. They appreciate you just that much more when they see you. I picked up my check and ambled to the cash register up front. The blonde followed, smiling. I counted out the change and slipped in an extra two-bits for her.

While she was ringing it up, I leaned over and ran two fingers lightly down her forearm. She crimsoned. "I'll see you again sometime," I said. "Maybe in the morning."

She smiled and nodded.

I was standing at the foot of the steps as Deb came hurrying through the revolving doors. She looked disappointed. She perked up at sight of me.

"There you are," she said. "I've been looking for you."

I saw her eyes brush up and down fast taking in my clothes. I could tell she hadn't seen many outfits like mine in this jerky town.

"What cooks?" I asked.

Her words spilled out like someone had pulled the cork. "Father's crazy about our idea of the memorial. He's having his secretary check into old estates that might be suitable. There are several that were built in the late Twenties that could be bought."

There had been a complete transition since yesterday. The dullness, the languor had left her eyes. With that red hair shining in the sunlight and that new radiance, she was really one gorgeous doll.

I said, "I was just on my way to the station. Thought maybe I could get a train out today for Philly."

Her face collapsed. When she looked up at me I saw a mist forming on her long lashes.

"Couldn't you ... stay a couple of days? Until we get the property bought anyway?"

I laid my hand on her shoulder. People surged around us and stared. "Well ... if you think I'd be any help...."

The lights went on again in her eyes. "You mean you will?"

"Sure. If you want me."

She became all business then. Took a small leather notebook from her purse. "First thing," she said happily, "we'll go down and you can meet Dad. He's such a peach. I know you'll like him."

She started steering me toward her car. "Next, we'll go over to McNulty's Real Estate office and check on what they have."

We slid into the car and started weaving through the traffic. She babbled every foot of the way. I looked interested.

All the time I was thinking of that little cream puff in the doughnut shop. *Jesus!* How she'd look in one of those sheer nightgowns I'd seen in Burdine's window ... Or even without one for that matter....

Deb hit the curbing with her front wheel and it snapped me back to attention. I looked at her and smiled. "This is your father's building?"

It was a swell pile of polished granite. Seven stories high. "This is the City Building," she said. "Dad's on the top floor."

The old man's sanctum was off by itself in one wing of the

building. Very special, I guess. It looked pretty drab to me. The golden oak chairs in the reception room were all filled with yokels looking like they'd lost their last friend. It had some tan drapes at the windows and a red carpet on the floor.

The old man's secretary looked up and gushed when we came in. Deb introduced me. The face was a fugitive from a tintype. Everybody in the room was looking at us as we breezed through the door marked "PRIVATE."

I'd been anxious to meet Owens. I knew I could scale him for size. You get good at that in my business. Well, I wasn't disappointed! He was a rabbit. Not the kind you find in the woods. The backyard variety. The kind that live in a store box with chicken wire across the front.

Small, slightly bald, pince-nez sitting uncertainly on his beezer. A smile like sticky candy. He shook my hand and gave me a line of guff about how swell it was of me to stop and see them. About what a fine thing the memorial would be for the underprivileged boys in the town. Of course, I agreed. All of a sudden he was serious. He lowered his voice.

"There's only one thing," he said. "You know how it is in public life. Unfortunately, there's always a certain element that question motives. Even though this project is purely charity ... still people might get the wrong impression if they thought the city manager or his family were behind it."

I knew he was thinking about those votes he might need in future elections. Politicians. They're all alike.

"Sure," I agreed. "I understand perfectly, Mr. Owens."

He laughed shortly. "Remember Al Capone's soup kitchens in Chicago during the depression? And Huey Long's University of Louisiana? We don't want our townspeople to get an impression we're trying to pull anything like that."

"I'm sure they wouldn't," I said vigorously. "Not with a record as fine as yours."

I saw him puff up like a toad. Nothing like soft butter for a biscuit like him. This baby was made to order for our game.

For a minute I had a start. Deb went around the desk. She threw her arm around his shoulder.

"Dad," she said, "if this memorial is in any way going to injure your career...."

The old man pulled her over and kissed her on the cheek.

"Now, now, none of that," he said. "It's just that we've never told anyone about the money from your mother's estate. It's quite a sum. Personally, I think it's very commendable for you to want to spend it so unselfishly. Later, after the memorial is going, it won't make any difference." He shot me a glance. "But for the time being, I think it's better if we keep the donor's name quiet."

I thought so too.

Owens took a slip of paper from his desk drawer and handed it to Deb. "This is the list of estates we looked up," he said. "You and Mr. Fagan here run over and talk to Ernest McNulty. He's expecting you." He motioned in the general direction of his reception room. "I have a lot of people to see."

We shook hands again and exchanged lies about how happy we were to know each other.

Back in Deb's car headed for the real estate office, I said, "Your dad is certainly a grand guy."

She brushed a warm smile over me. "I'm awfully glad you think so. I knew you two would like each other."

"How do you know he liked me?"

"I can tell in a second when Dad likes anyone. He's as transparent as glass when you know him."

I silently agreed with her there. I'd only known him for ten minutes and I'd bet a century note I could read off his pedigree like the one my bull terrier used to have.

Out of the corner of my eye I caught the satisfied smile on her face. The streets were crowded and we drove slowly up Main and made a left at Sixth. People passing gave us the eye. A lot of them waved at Deb. I could see she was top drawer in that town.

We parked in front of the real estate office. It was a long, low white building, with a green tile roof and McNulty's name smeared in big block letters across the window. I helped Deb out of the car and followed her into the reception room.

A typewriter stopped clacking and a trim-looking brunette lifted gorgeous brown eyes. Deb said we wanted to see Mr.

McNulty. The girl forced a bored smile and told us to sit down while she did a disappearing act into his office. A minute later she was back and ushered us in.

There are times in my business when it's hard as hell to keep from laughing. This was one of them. This McNulty guy should have given himself to the old-fats drive! All he needed was a white cotton beard to make a perfect department store Santa Claus! He had everything else. The bay window, the pink cheeks, the belly laugh. When I shook his hand it was like soft lard.

He said, "I'm very happy to meet you," looking me straight in the eye. "Owens called me about the memorial. I think it's the greatest thing that ever happened to Hart City."

I thought so too.

I smiled at Deb. "I don't deserve any credit," I said modestly.

He patted me on the back. "I know," he said, "and Owens cautioned me about keeping the entire transaction a secret."

We took chairs. Fatso leaned back expansively behind his desk. His eyes were taking me in. I was bored and wanted to get on with the deal. I could see though he was dying for a load of hero talk.

He said, "They tell me you were in the thick of it."

I nodded. Looked at the rug.

"What outfit were you with?"

I could feel my scalp prickle. I was loaded for him. Nevertheless I didn't like tight corners.

"530th, Armored Infantry." I said it fast.

"Headquarters Company?"

"Yes."

He rocked forward in his chair. Looked happy. I didn't like it. He said, "You must have known my nephew then. Bob McNulty?"

I shot Deb a glance. It was written all over her face she expected me to say yes.

While I was still deciding whether to take the bait, McNulty rumbled. "You probably might not know him by that name. Everyone called him 'Fisheye.'"

I decided to take the plunge. I knew by the way he was

talking the punk was dead.

I brightened. "Fisheye," I said. "Good old Fisheye. Sure, I knew him all right."

McNulty and Deb both seemed pleased for a minute. Then Deb threw in a bomb. "But Jim wrote me that Fisheye was transferred out of that outfit before they went overseas. He was killed on Wake." She was looking at me like I'd stolen her blind.

A chill slid down my back. At the same time the room got hotter than hell. I made a fast mental shuffle of my outs and picked the best. There was a hole in it you could drive an elephant through. But I had to take a chance.

I said, "I didn't mean I knew him personally." I kept my voice low and steady. I pulled out the stop marked "with feeling," looked Fatso straight in the eye. "Ever soldier?" I asked.

He said no.

"You don't know what it is then to be out there in those jungles week after week, month after month, wet, half sick and discouraged. Wondering every second if you're going to be next. You get to know a lot of people even though you've never really seen them. You read the other guy's mail when you don't get any. You talk for hours with him about his home and friends...."

I choked up. Deb was brushing a tear out of her eye.

McNulty's smile slid off his face. He looked like he was going to cry. I knew he was putting me down as a case of battle fatigue.

It was quiet in the room for a second. Then I said, "I've heard Jim talk so much about Fisheye. It's like I knew him better than a lot of people I really do know."

McNulty said he understood. He cleared his throat and got down to business.

I breathed a sigh of relief. Jesus! That was too close for comfort. Sometimes I wished Silky had this job up his....

McNulty had the floor and he was covering it like a rug. He was telling about each estate on the list. Giving a glowing description of the houses, the grounds, the taxes, the sale price. He talked about several, but he always worked back to one. He said it was an Italian villa built by some count or duke or something. According to him it was just what the doctor ordered. Seaview Villa, he called it. Ten acres of land, swimming pool, stables, tennis courts, a clubhouse built in the woods. Just the place for some of the boys' classes! He wasn't using a trowel, he was laying it on with a steam shovel!

After he almost finished he mentioned the price and went right on talking. ONE HUNDRED GRAND! No wonder he had a fever over this place. Think of the commission. I'll bet he'd never made a sale like that!

I was getting itchy. Thought if he didn't stop blabbing I'd get up and give him a poke. I get like that sometimes. My throat felt like cotton. Sweat was sticky in the palms of my hands. I knew I'd blow my top in a second.

McNulty paused to get his breath.

I said, "I wonder if I could have a drink of water?"

He smiled. "Sure, there's a cooler in the outer office."

I got out of there just in time. Shut the door behind me. Glamourpuss was still pounding on her typewriter. She didn't even glance up. I went over to the corner and ran a drink in a paper cup. I could hear her fingers slowing on her typewriter. Feel her eyes boring into my back. I knew she'd like to know me better.

Without turning, I said, "Hi, New York."

Her typewriter stopped. "What did you say?"

"Or is it Chicago?"

I turned then and she was all smiles.

"How did you know?" she asked.

"I know Bergdorf Goodman when I see it. You're not from this weed patch."

She looked interested. "It is New York. You're pretty good at calling your shots."

I said, "I'm good at a lot of things. One of them is reading minds." I moved close to her desk. "You're fed to the teeth with this town. I could tell it the minute I walked in."

I was giving her the once-over. She had light brown hair parted in the center and a big roll at the nape of her neck. She was built on rangy lines but the slick tailored suit made them look swell. She wore no rouge but bright red lips.

"You don't look like a local product yourself," she said.

"Philadelphia and New York."

She brightened. "Going back soon?"

"About a week—I hope."

She ran a red fingernail across the spacer on her typewriter. "Me, too," she said. "They can give this place back to the Spaniards."

I knew she was waiting for me to ask for her New York address. I didn't tumble. I just kept looking at her.

"Since I've been in this whistle stop," she said, "I'd almost forgotten there were men like you...."

I leaned over the desk and grinned at her. I said softly, "Maybe I can help you remember."

Then I heard it. The door from McNulty's office opened with a soft click. I yanked my head around. Deb was standing there looking at me. She didn't look pleased.

She said, "Did you have to dig a well for that water?"

Santa Claus came hurrying right out behind her. I caught up with them at the door.

"Where do we go now?" I asked Deb.

She was all business. "Out to Seaview Villa," she said.

"That's great," I grinned at McNulty. Santa Claus, I thought, was right on the ball. That wasn't a bad job of roping.

## Chapter 7

We were all three in the front seat of McNulty's Packard rolling down the coastal highway. A verdant range of bulky mountains swept up on our right. Fatso pointed to a pink blurb about halfway up that nestled against the green mountainside. "Seaview Villa."

He swerved the car to the right and we started climbing a typical mountain road. The car was laboring in second gear. "It's exactly a mile and a quarter from the highway to the house," McNulty said. Apparently the road hadn't been used for a long time. Scrub oak and firs reached grasping fingers as the big car nosed branches out of the way.

We made a sharp left turn and emerged with startling suddenness from the thicket. Before us stood two massive columns of pink stone holding elaborate wrought-iron gates. A heavy log chain and padlock held the gates against intruders.

McNulty stopped the car and struggled out from under the wheel. He tried several keys before the lock snapped. After he had opened the gates he came puffing back to the car. He looked as if he were about to take the count with apoplexy from that minor exertion. He mopped his face and neck before we started up the long u-shaped driveway.

What an igloo! There it was right ahead of us. I thought I'd seen some swanky wigwams in Miami, but nothing like this! It made Hetty Green's place look like an outhouse. The main building was of the same pink stone as the gate columns. The roof of white, glazed tile sparkled in the sunlight.

Weeds had taken over where the lawns used to be but even this didn't detract from the house. It was like a fine oil painting, dimmed a little with age.

Santa Claus had found his breath again. He parked the car and we all piled out. He started a long spiel about the fine points of the place. How the stone had been imported from the Old Country to the tune of a hundred G's. We were walking around just looking. I wasn't even listening to the line of guff he was putting out. I don't think Deb was either. Her face was all lights and soft music.

Even after months of neglect the box hedges in the formal garden showed genius of design. Roses, red, yellow and white, were blooming in profusion. Fountains of white marble supported delicately carved figures of lovely women in a most delectable state of nudity. One of them reminded me of a girl I used to know in St. Louis. Or maybe it was Kansas City. Anyway, she had personality with a sack over her face.

A sharp breeze was blowing from the ocean, rattling the shaggy heads of royal palm trees. Far below, a white crescent of sand marked the private beach. We saw the blue-tiled swimming pool, the stables, the tennis courts, the greenhouse. I had just begun to wonder when Fatso would get unwound. We were walking on the north side of the property when he wilted onto a bench and started his mopping again.

"Whew! Hot, isn't it?"

I nodded.

He smiled apologetically. "Why don't you two just roam around by yourselves for a while? It's the best way to make up your minds anyway. I'll sit here and rest."

He tossed me the key to the house.

"This fits the rear door," he said. "After you give the house the once-over take the path through the woods to the clubhouse."

We went through the place. Deb was all eyes. It was a sight! Marble floors like giant checkerboards, friezes so delicately carved they looked like lace, wall niches everywhere, a fireplace in every room, French windows opening on loggias with a view of the sea.

Deb kept saying the same thing over and over again. "It's lovely!" She didn't just say it in the usual way. She breathed it with reverence. Like a preacher says "Amen" in church. I knew she'd made up her mind. I didn't want to put on the bite. After all, it wasn't anything to me. I did agree with her and once I said, "I think this is an ideal place." She smiled and looked up at me. Her eyes were saying she thought so too.

When we came out, I locked the door. We started down the path through the woods. It was quiet except for the chatter of birds and the distant booming of the surf. Sunshine filtered through the giant trees and fell in golden flakes along the path. I had her hand in mine. It was soft and warm and I could feel the rapid beating of her pulse.

We reached a clearing and saw the clubhouse. It was made of stripped redwood logs. We didn't have a key but looked in through the windows. There were four large rooms, each with a stone fireplace in the end. We discussed briefly how ideal the place would be for classes, picnic suppers, a general recreational center for the boys.

After that, we wandered on kind of aimlessly. The path wove in and out among the trees. I felt a certain rapture I knew was part of the play. Things were going right. Deb had clammed up but it wasn't because she was bored. She was on fire inside. Her cheeks were flushed and her eyes shining.

As we walked along I kept watching her from the corner of my eye. She had taken off the jacket to her suit and carried it over her arm. I could see the rapid rise and fall of her breasts under the tight enclosure of her white Angora sweater.

I don't know how long we walked, maybe ten or fifteen minutes, when we came to another clearing. It was cool and quiet. There was a narrow mountain stream rushing over shiny rocks. A fallen tree someone had fixed for a bridge. Deb sat down on it and ran her fingers through her hair. I sat down beside her.

Neither of us talked for a minute. I was taking her in. She was really beautiful when you saw her like this. The smooth clearness of her skin, the wide-set eyes. The frail wisps of red-gold hair caressing her neck and shoulders in the wind. I wondered if Jim Clark had really known what a delectable dish he had.

I doubted it. Dopes like that—the psalm-singing kind—are always out trying to help somebody else instead of helping themselves.

Her voice brought me out of it.

"I'm happier today than I've been for a long time, Rick."

I smiled down at her. "I'm glad," I said.

She was so close to me, I could feel her breathing. A faint

perfume rose from her hair. Her eyes looked dreamy.

"It's hard to explain," she said, "but today while we were going through the house, I had the strangest feeling. As if Jim were with us—the three of us walking along together...."

I said with feeling, "I know what you mean." Jesus, I did, too! I'd been haunted by this defunct boy scout ever since I hit this burg, hadn't I?

Somewhere in the brush a small animal scurried for cover. A sea gull wheeled against the blue overhead. The surf boomed in the distance.

Deb was staring into space. There were neon lights in her eyes. She was absent-mindedly turning her ring around on her finger.

I remembered the newspaper clipping in the envelope Silky had given me. A write-up about her engagement party. It had given a big buildup to this star ruby.

I took her left hand in mine and studied the ring. "It's beautiful," I said. "Jim's mother's, wasn't it, and he had it reset for you?"

Her eyes brimmed with surprise. "Jim told you?" I nodded.

"You must have been very close." She said it to herself. I still had her hand in mine. I pressed it.

She was breathing more rapidly now. I could feel the soft warm flesh of her thigh against mine. Oh, God, how easy it would be ... nobody would ever know ... Fatso wasn't within hearing distance. The hot blood throbbed at my temple ... my palms were moist and sticky. My arm reached for her.

Then a signal flashed through my brain. Fagan, have you gone nuts? Don't throw a curve now and curdle the play. You're no schoolboy on the make. I had to talk to myself like hell to come around. This is a nice girl. No round-heeled frump that can be pushed over with a feather. Somehow I came down out of the clouds.

I released her hand and stood up. "I think we'd better be going," I said. "Santa Claus might not like it if we stayed away too long."

She laughed. "You mean Mr. McNulty?"

"Sure. Doesn't he look like Old Saint Nick?"

"Come to think of it, he does," she smiled.

We walked faster on the way back to Seaview Villa than we had on the way out. My watch said we'd been gone almost an hour. I knew Deb didn't have any idea of the time.

She babbled all the way back about the memorial, just how the house could be fixed. I nodded politely in the right places but my mind had slid away from Deb Clark, the memorial and even Hart City. I was thinking of Tory. Nights that we'd spent together. Her supple body pressed close against mine. Her hot breath on my neck. Christ, what I wouldn't give for a night with her right now!

My mind was possessed with the thought. Silky had said she'd left Miami by plane last night. I rapidly calculated the time. She could be in Hart City tonight. I'd be watched, I knew that. But I knew Tory too. If she ever hit town she'd find a way of giving Silky's goons the slip and getting to me.

As we approached across the sweep of lawn, McNulty saw us and stood up. "Well, did you see everything?"

"Yes, everything," Deb said, "It's a lovely spot."

On the way back to town nobody talked much. I kept watching Deb. She was getting a hell of a reaction from our little séance in the woods.

Fatso drove straight to his office. As we climbed into Deb's car, she told him she'd let him know in a day or so about the property.

He said, "Take all the time you want." But I knew by the look on his pan he was busting to get her name on the dotted line.

She dropped me off at the Y. I promised to call her later.

As soon as I stepped inside the door, I knew the heat was on. A rat-faced little guy, with a toothpick jutting from the corner of his mouth, was sprawled in a lounge chair making like he was reading the paper. I recognized him as one of the goons Silky had picked up in Miami. He didn't give me a tumble and I walked right past him to the desk. Charley was looking confused.

I knew my lines from here. "Say, Charley, I'm expecting my brother sometime today. If he should show up...."

Charley broke in, beaming relief. "He's waiting in your room,

Rick."

"Fine," I said and started toward the elevator.

"Oh, Rick...."

I hid a smile as I turned back. I'd been expecting this.

Charley leaned across the desk. His tone was confidential. "I was a little worried when your brother asked to wait up there. We have a rule against giving out keys, and you two don't look a bit alike. Maybe I was a little short with him. I hope you'll extend my apologies."

I said it was my fault for not telling him I was expecting company.

When I opened the door of my room, Max Graber was sitting over by the window doing the crossword puzzle in the paper. I got a kick out of it. No wonder Charley had failed to see the resemblance. Max used to be a professional pug. Now he could pass as a banker. His pan was ugly enough, but somehow he had a way of wearing his expensive clothes, a way of talking to suckers that was smooth and convincing.

A cigar slanted from his lips. He didn't turn his head.

"Silky thought you might be lonesome," he said quietly without lifting his eyes from the paper. "You know how he is about keeping all the boys happy."

"Sure, sure, I know. Damned white of him. What do we do, play drop the handkerchief?"

Max laughed. "I like spin the milk bottle best."

I pulled off my coat and tie. "I'm taking a shower if you don't mind. If you do mind, you can go to hell."

I finished stripping off my clothes and went into the bathroom leaving the door open.

"Women cause all the trouble in this world," Max called in conversationally.

"You thinking of one in particular?"

"Maybe in your case."

"Does she have black hair?"

"Maybe." Max hesitated, then said, "Chrissake, I don't understand the boss. If a woman doesn't go for a guy what the hell's the use of trying to hold her?"

I knew then what the game was. Tory had hit town. Max had

cabled Havana, tipped her off where we were. Now he was trying to shake me down for her address. I knew damn well he'd held out on Silky but thought I'd be good for a bite. He wasn't touching me. If Tory was in Hart City she'd figure out a way of getting her address to me—and fast. I took my shower. Halfway through, I heard someone knock on the outside door. Then a low murmur of voices as Max talked to the visitor.

Still dripping, I sauntered out into the room. Max was going through an opened package on the chair like a terrier.

He grinned sheepishly when he saw me. "Orders is orders."

"My stuff from the drugstore." I said it nonchalantly, as if I'd been expecting it all the time.

I glanced through the contents. It consisted of a twenty-five-cent murder mystery novel, a package of cigarettes, and a bottle of Alka-Seltzer.

Max said, "It's all yours. I gave it the once-over and if there's a note concealed in that junk, I'm a monkey's uncle."

I said, "What have you got against monkeys?"

He ignored the remark and went back to his crossword puzzle.

I started for the bathroom. "I'm sure glad this medicine came," I said. "I've had a headache all afternoon."

Max grunted.

The water rushed into the washbowl as I unscrewed the cap from the Alka-Seltzer, removed the wad of cotton, picked a note the size of a postage stamp from the top tablet. It read: 2265 Ocean Drive—that was all. I rolled it into a small ball and let it wash down the bowl.

I was getting one hell of a lift out of putting this over on Silky and Max. I knew how much Tory would enjoy it, too, when I saw her tonight. That Tory was a genius when it came to figuring angles. She was probably across the street in the drugstore when I came in. Spotted the goon in the lobby and knew Silky would have another parked in my room. She bought the stuff, made an excuse to use the telephone, taking the Alka-Seltzer bottle with her, wrote the note, slipped it into the bottle, then had the stuff sent up. I could just see the little wench working it all out!

I knew it was dangerous, having her in town. But right then

I didn't give a damn.

I finished dressing and started for the door.

Max snarled. "Where you going?"

"For a walk, sweetheart. You'll have to spin the milk bottle alone. Check all phone calls and packages. Isn't that what Silky said?"

"Shut up."

I breezed out the door.

At first I didn't see the goon when I went through the lobby. But just as I reached the revolving door, I saw his back lounging against a pillar by the entrance. He gave me the eye when I went past. I turned into the doughnut shop. The place was almost full. Beautiful gave me a wink as I headed for a stool at the back. She finished waiting on a couple of palookas and sailed up to me. She was all smiles. "Morning came fast," she giggled.

I wasn't in a mood for humor. I kept shifting my eyes toward the big plate glass window in the front. The goon was marching slowly up and down. Keeping an eye on me. I noticed there was about ten seconds between his trips.

I said low, "Where does that back door go?"

Beautiful looked puzzled. "Out into the Y.M.C.A. parking lot. Why?"

I shifted my eyes to the front window again. The goon had just gone by.

"Because I have to meet a fellow out there."

I slid off the stool and beat it out the back door. I saw my rented car parked across the lot. I headed for it, glancing around every couple seconds to see if I was being tailed. I wasn't. I slid into the Pontiac, ground the starter and shot out on the main street. Ocean Drive I knew was north of town on the Coastal Highway.

## Chapter 8

Night falls like a curtain in California. When I left the parking lot the sky overhead was a dirty grey, streaked with bright orange ribbons. By the time I reached the edge of town, darkness had moved in. Windows in low, huddling houses were squares of pale yellow. The surf pounded heavily along the highway. A stiff wind carried a damp chill as it sifted in around the car window. I stopped in a filling station to ask directions. The attendant told me 2265 Ocean Drive was a mile or so up the beach. I couldn't miss it. It was an old shingle shack, standing by itself, on the beach side of the road in a clump of fir trees. I lighted a cigarette and wheeled out of the station.

My eyes flicked nervously between the road ahead and the rearview mirror. A pair of bright headlights gleamed a few hundred feet behind me. I wondered if I was dragging a tail. I slowed to twenty and watched. The car kept coming. Then it passed me. I felt relieved.

Slowly my senses were returning. I was cooling on this Tory deal. It was too damn dangerous. I must have been cracked to think I could get by with it. Sooner or later Silky would find out. Then there'd be hell to pay. I'd made up my mind. I'd give her enough cash to get back to Miami. She could hole in there until after the fix was solid. Maybe I could send for her then.

I knew she'd be like a wildcat when I told her, but what the devil.... I'd been through scenes with her before.... I could handle her all right.

I'd come a mile and two-tenths. I knew I was almost there. The car was idling along slowly. A white probing finger of light from my spot skipped along the beach side of the highway, picked up thickening clumps of trees, finally the shack 2265 sat in the shadows twenty feet from the beach. Giant northern fir trees towered over it. The shades were drawn, but on either side thin ribbons of light escaped. I snapped off my lights and turned into the dark garage. The car rolled to a stop. I jerked the ignition key and climbed out. Just as a safety measure, I closed the garage doors.

A board creaked as I stepped onto the porch. From inside I could hear the music of a dance band playing softly on the radio. The thin tinkle of ice. Tory was mixing highballs.

The door was unlocked. I opened it slowly. There was only one lamp burning in the room. The air was heavy with the pungent odor of burning wood. A small fire struggled in the fireplace, throwing jagged lights and shadows. Tory didn't move. She had her back to me still mixing drinks. I shut the door.

She didn't turn. "Took you long enough." There was a chill in her voice.

"Start talking," I said, "and fast."

Her hands stopped in mid-air clenching the Seltzer bottle.

"That's a helluva way to greet a girl who's come across the continent to see you."

I said, "I oughta bust in that pretty face of yours. You know the rules when a play's on."

She turned and started toward me.

The firelight did something to her face. It erased the harshness and left a smooth, white oval. Slight blue shadows of fatigue showed under the dark velvet of her eyes. It softened her, made her look younger.

Folds in the white satin house coat shimmered in the dancing light as it fell around her voluptuous body. A low-cut, square neck revealed the fullness of her breasts. The sun in Miami had left her skin the color of coffee.

She kept coming toward me. Slowly. She was smiling now. Her white teeth flashing. Her rounded arms encircled my neck and pulled me to her. Her face was a mask of mockery as her eyes met mine. She said softly, "You're a mean son-of-a-bitch, Rick, but I love you."

Her full, red lips were parted slightly. I could feel her hot breath against my face. Fire was seering through my veins. I started to kiss her.

She twisted out of my arms and stepped away. She laughed harshly. "But I don't like phonies who give me the brush, see? So run along. I've got bigger fish on the line."

I could have slapped the hell out of her right then. Inside I was burning. I tried to choke it. I walked over to the fireplace and took my time lighting a cigarette. When I turned she has spread that lovely torso of hers on the divan. Her house coat had fallen away on one smooth shoulder. Firelight danced provocatively in her eyes.

I said, "Seen Silky?"

"Christ, no." For an instant raw fear flooded her eyes. She tried to cover it. Then she laughed again. That harsh, grating laugh. "You know damn well I haven't. If you thought for a minute that Silky knew I was in town you wouldn't come within a mile of this place."

I looked at her hard. "How do you know you can trust Max? He's been known to stool before."

She lighted a cigarette.

"You wouldn't stool if the other guy held all the aces."

"Meaning?"

"Wouldn't Silky like to hear that Max cabled me in Havana?"

"Still it must have cost you plenty. Max isn't playing for gum wrappers."

She tossed her head, her black hair swept her shoulders. "Remember the score we took from the Indiana sucker last winter?"

I nodded.

"Maybe Max got greedy and held out some of the take." She laughed again. "Tory gets around, sweetheart, and sometimes overhears things that come in handy...."

"I get it." I walked over to the divan and sat down beside her. I said, "Listen, baby, I think you're tops, just like I always have, but Silky thinks so, too. As long as he's running this show I'm stringing along, see?"

I tried to put my arm around her. She threw it away. Her eyes were flashing. She straightened and looked at me.

"Get this straight, handsome, I ain't a piece of real estate. Nobody buys and sells Tory." Her eyes narrowed dangerously. "I'm through with Silky Angelo—washed up—I don't ever want his greasy hands to touch me." She was breathing faster.

I didn't answer for a minute. The only sound was the soft music from the radio and the surf pounding angrily on the beach. "The point is," I said quietly, "he isn't through with you. Coming here tonight I took a hell of a chance. I don't know now about a tail. Maybe someone's waiting out there, laying for me. Or on his way back to report to Silky."

She moved closer. Looked scared. "What are you trying to tell me?"

"That we have a couple of drinks together, then I take you to the Vista Del Mar and turn you over to Silky."

I stiffened and waited for the explosion. Instead, one of her hands reached for my coat lapel and pulled me to her. For a long time I bent and kissed her. Her lips were soft and yielding. I forgot Silky. Danger was only a word in the dictionary.

Suddenly she pulled away from me and jumped up. She went over to the table and brought our drinks. When she was curled up against me again, sipping hers, she said, "Let's forget everything for tonight, Rick. Just let it be you and me...." I agreed with her. I liked it. I kissed her again hard and took another pull at my drink.

For a while we sat without talking. Watching the red tongues of flame in the fireplace. After a while I asked, "How was Havana?"

"That hellhole," she said angrily. "Goddamn that Silky. He cabled the money directly to the hotel for my room and only let me have enough for eats. Said it would keep me out of trouble."

I brushed a hand across her forehead. "Did it?"

She threw back her head and laughed. I laughed with her. When she stopped, she said, "You know Tory. I could stir up something in the middle of the Sahara."

"Who was the guy?"

Our glasses were empty. "I'll tell you about it." She crossed to the table for a refill. She came back with fresh highballs, sat down and snuggled against me again.

"Some Joe from Texas," she said.

"Grifter?"

"Small-time. Pretty good operator at that. Knew lots of angles."

I looked down at her. "Curves, too, eh?"

She kissed me.

Suddenly she burst out laughing. She laughed until tears glistened on the long, dark sweep of her lashes.

"What's so funny?" I asked.

"I met this oyster one night at the bar. He sized me up in a hurry. I danced with him. When I said I was from St. Paul he asked me if I knew Sid Gleason. That was the tip-off."

I said, "That ain't funny."

She kissed me again.

"From there on it got funny. We made a bet. He said the tourists down there were so damn jerky he'd bet me a century we could pull off the engineer's daughter."

"No foolin'?"

She nodded. "We were both kind of tight by then. I went to work on a retired croaker from Dodge City, Iowa. I spotted him at the bar. There was an empty stool side of him. I managed to hit his elbow just as he was taking a drink. The drink showered me. He started blubbering about how sorry he was and I told him it was okay and laughed it off. He offered to buy me a new dress. We had a few more drinks. He was loaded. I said I'd have to go to my room and change before I took pneumonia. He insisted on going with me. I kept saying no dice and dragging him right along." She threw back her head and laughed again.

"I'm way ahead of you," I said. "The Texas monkey knocks at the door. He's your father. He's madder than hell. You pull off a shakedown and it works."

That Tory was a card. I was enjoying it.

"For eight centuries, it works," she said. "How'd you think I bought my airplane ticket?"

"I hadn't thought. I know you."

The liquor was getting to us. I could feel numbness in my lips. I was in a glorious state of suspension. The light from the fireplace had died out. Only a dull red glow shone from the embers. I could smell the spicy perfume in Tory's hair. She knew I was almost wacky for her.

She said softly, "You're not going to send me away?"

It was like a cold shower of water hitting me in the face. It brought me back to my senses.

I said, "Baby, I can't let you spoil the play." I pulled away from her.

Before I could stop her she sprang to her feet, eyes blazing. She went to the fireplace, whirled on me and yelled, "I know what play I'm spoiling. You cheap double-dealing bastard. I saw you this afternoon from across the street. You and that redheaded bitch coming out of a real estate office. I know what you're trying to pull. I found a picture of her in your pocket in Miami."

I tried to keep my voice low and even. "Don't be a chump. She's part of the play."

That stopped her.

"How's that?"

"You know what would happen to me if Silky ever found out I'd spilled my guts about a play."

She nodded. Small lines creased her forehead. She said, "I've got a right to know."

"Okay, but keep your trap shut. She's the daughter of the city manager of Hart City. We're framing the girl, then getting an airtight fix from her old man to get her out of the jam."

Tory didn't look convinced. "Sounds corny to me."

I talked fast. "Americans love corn. You said so yourself not five minutes ago. If they didn't, do you think they'd still fall for the engineer's daughter?"

"Where do you fit in?" she wanted to know.

"I'm a pal of her dead husband's on my way back from the South Pacific. I'm just stopping off here to give her his dying words. After I get her built up, I'll lead her to slaughter."

Tory came back and sank down beside me. "Christ, and I can remember when con men were clever."

"A lot depends on the groundwork."

"You mean that was good?"

"Silky sent a smart cookie out here from Miami two months ago. He did a swell job. Everything is perfect. That's why I say we can't gum the play."

"You're sure Silky isn't trying to marry you off to the dame? That might put in the fix and also get you off my neck. Ever think of that?"

"Sure," I lied. "I've thought of it but that isn't the deal. Silky isn't throwing his best roper to the wolves for just one play. Anyway, he knows there's no storm and strife for me."

Tory bared her teeth in a humorless smile. "There hadn't better be," she said. "And if that redhead tries to bust us up, I'll kill her surer than hell."

"You keep your claws off that redhead," I said. "She's a nice girl. She wouldn't understand the way you play."

This burned her. She hauled off and slapped me hard across the mouth. I slapped her back. She slumped down onto the divan and began to cry.

I turned off the lamp and the radio and went over and sat beside her. I told her I was sorry. She said to get out. I kissed her; it was a salty kiss. There wasn't a sound but our breathing. That and the pounding of the surf outside....

It was almost midnight when I left Tory's. It was hell pulling myself away. Driving back to town along the dark, windswept highway, I got to thinking. Maybe I was a chump always playing so goddamned safe. I thought there might be talk around the Y if I stayed out any later. The last movie house closed at twelve. Any spot staying open later in Hart City was strictly undercover.

I guess I was still too groggy from the drinks to notice. Anyway, I swung into the parking lot. It was pitch-black. Suddenly, I saw it. Almost riding my bumper was a pair of powerful, low-slung headlights. I caught them in the rearview mirror. God knows how long they'd been there. I'd been tailed from Tory's! My heart did a swan dive. I pulled up and parked, setting my hand brake. Then I heard the smooth, even purr of Silky's grey Continental as it pulled up slowly beside me. In the dim light from the dash I could see the outline of Max Graber at the wheel. He was alone. I froze in the seat.

Rolling down the car window, he called to me, "Hey, Rick, how about taking a little ride?"

I got out of the car slowly. My legs felt weak. I was struggling to keep my voice even. I said, "Some other time. I'm tired as hell." I knew there was a catch. The quicker I found out what it was the better. Max's big head was thrust out the car window.

His voice tightened. "That's orders. Silky wants to see you."

I slid in beside him. He drove west out of town, turned south on the Coastal Highway. Neither of us were talking. I knew it was the blow-off. All the way I was trying to stop my nerves from jumping. He pulled up and stopped at a crummy-looking beer joint. There was only one old battered car outside. No lights showed at the windows. A raw, cold wind whipped at us from the ocean across the highway.

When we opened the door the sour smell of stale grease and beer mixed with cigarette smoke choked us. The place was only dimly lighted. I didn't see anyone but a fat, sleepy bartender, draped over the far end of the bar. He didn't even move his head. Only his bloodshot eyes followed us. Max led the way. We went back through the joint to a private room. Silky and Dice were sitting behind a table looking grim. A bright, naked light bulb hung from the ceiling. They glanced up as we came through the door. Max said, "I'll wait in the car, Chief." He left.

I felt the ice tightening along my spine. I was wondering how to play it. Maybe it was sort of a nervous hysteria. Anyway, for a minute I had a notion to just yell out that sure, I'd seen Tory, been with her all evening, and what the hell were they going to do about it? But I didn't. One thing stopped me. Silky's hands were under the table. He could have had a heater.

Smoothly Silky said, "Sit down, Rick, we want to talk to you."

I sat.

For a minute that seemed like a week he didn't say anything. Then finally he cleared his throat. His voice was gruff. "We've got some good news for you."

I let out a breath of relief. I felt like a kid on Christmas morning.

"What gives?"

He slid a Havana from his vest pocket. Carefully trimmed the end with a gold pocketknife and shoved it in the corner of his mouth. He said,

"A couple of days ago I leased an old, broken-down oil refinery up the coast. It hasn't been operated for years. Anyway, it's a swell convincer. I'm having it painted. The boys are fixing up the boilers so we can have steam pouring out for the benefit of the suckers. Tomorrow we open an office in Hart City. We'll peddle the stock around L. A. If the slobs get skeptical we'll bring them up to see the plant."

"What if they want to go through?" I asked.

Silky laughed and rolled the cigar to the other corner of his mouth. "I've thought of that, too. There's a six-foot, barbed-wire fence around the place and signs, 'KEEP OUT. SECRET WORK.' The tale is we're working on government stuff. Nobody is allowed inside."

"Pretty cagey." I nodded.

Suddenly Silky's pan went serious. "There's only one thing. I'd like to have this local fix in before we actually start the play. Money's easy now. Suckers a dime a dozen. With the local boys fixed we can take off our score before anyone gets wise. The local Chamber of Commerce will recommend us. We'll look legitimate as hell. Isn't that Clark dame ready for the frame yet?"

I hesitated. Stalled a minute for time. "Not yet," I said. "Give me a couple of more days."

I knew Silky didn't like it.

"It's tough trying to hold the boys," he complained. "You know how they get when there's nothing to do. Besides, my payroll's pretty heavy."

"I'll do my best," I said. "Don't try to rush things. You know how easy it is to blow the works."

Silky nodded and touched a match to his cigar.

## Chapter 9

For the next few days even living at the Y didn't bother me. Nothing bothered me. Not even Charley Meyer's dopey amenities when I met him in the lobby. I was too damned exhausted most of the time to care where I was or what happened. This Deb Clark had more enthusiasm than a fraternity pledge in a corn-belt college. Her spirit was what literary guys call indefatigable.

Her father had felt that she might be able to find a place less expensive than Seaview Villa, so she was looking over every available property within twenty miles of Hart City. I tramped around estates and talked about the memorial until I thought I'd go off my button.

The worst of it was Fatso almost always tagged along with us. I began to feel like a Siamese triplet.

Nights I'd drop out to Tory's I'd be so dog-tired and on edge we'd end up in a row.

"God, I'm a lucky dame! Sit in this stinking matchbox all day so I can listen to you snore all evening!"

"Okay. I'll stay at the Y a couple of nights and catch up on my sleep."

A funny look crossed her face—funny for Tory. "You try it!" she yelled. "This hole is bad enough in the daytime...." A shiver tightened her.

"Every time the damn thing rattles after dark, I get the jitters."

I went out to my car and got my automatic from the glove compartment. She didn't want to take it. She had a phobia against firearms. Which was just as good—with a temper like hers.

She lashed out at me when I yawned. "Why in hell don't you tell this raggle you're through with tramping over the back forty?"

"Swell con man you'd make," I sneered. "When you build up your mark you play along with what *she* wants to do."

"Well, what the hell *does* she want to do—train you for marathons?"

I was patient. "Remember, baby, I'm supposed to be a returned soldier. I eat up twenty-mile hikes before breakfast, with a sixty-pound pack on my back." I thought Tory would bust a hamstring laughing.

"Jesus, if that ain't a hot one! The Featherbed Kid, as phony a 4F as ever beat a draft rap, gets his basic training in three days with a sucker!"

I gave her a slap across the fanny.

But on the afternoon of the fifth day I bogged down. We were going through an old place called High Point. It sat on a bluff overlooking the ocean. Fatso had given out hours before. He was waiting for us in the car. We were going through the garden. I spotted a bench and steered Deb for it. After I'd pulled her down beside me, I said, "There's something I want to talk to you about."

She looked at me kind of worried.

"You look tired," I said. "I think you've overdone this house hunting."

She admitted she was tired.

I said, "I know you want to be thorough, but it seems to me we've seen enough."

"You're probably right. Which of the places we've seen today do you like the best?"

I made like I was thinking. What I wanted to say was I didn't give a good goddamn. Instead I said, "I can't see the Mexican place at all. It's colorful and all that, but somehow it just doesn't seem the right setting for a bunch of boys."

"How about the English manor house?"

Slowly I shook my head. "That's better," I said. "Still, with all that dark walnut paneling it struck me as a little gloomy."

"Funny," she mused aloud. "No matter how many places we see we always come back to Seaview Villa."

I picked up her hand and patted it absently. She didn't take it away.

"I think you're too tired to decide right now. Why don't we

celebrate with a little dinner tonight, and talk the whole thing over?"

Lights went on in her eyes. She liked the idea. She said, "Let's dress, just for fun, and go to the Spa."

"Where's that?"

"Up in the hills. It's beautiful. People drive all the way up from L.A. because of the food and the atmosphere."

I could see now I was getting somewhere. This walkathon we'd been carrying on for days wasn't the setting for romance. Take a dame at night in a filmy evening dress, soft music, softer lights ... hell, then a guy can make some time....

My wristwatch said ten minutes after seven when I finished dressing. The midnight-blue, double-breasted dinner jacket I'd paid two centuries for on Bond Street never let me down. The exercise of the past few days had rubbed off the slight trace of belly I picked up in Miami. My immaculate white shirt front and maroon bow tie (Sulka's in Chicago) accentuated my smooth, even tan. "Fagan," I said to myself, "as long as there are men like you, girls are bound to leave home."

Charley Meyer grinned at me from behind the desk when I went through the lobby. I knew what he was thinking. That I gave a tone to his joint. The average run of punks that stopped at the Y were about as colorful as a Quaker funeral.

I walked west two blocks to a florist shop and picked up a yellow orchid. Back at the parking lot I climbed into the Pontiac and drove out to Deb's. The maid steered me into the large living room, telling me all the way that Miss Deborah wasn't quite ready. The room was in semi-darkness. The maid snapped on a table lamp, smiled at me, and gumshoed toward the kitchen. I sat down and fiddled with a string on the glassine florist box until I heard light footsteps padding down the stairway.

I stood up when Deb sailed into the room. For a minute she took my breath away. She looked beautiful tonight. In an ethereal sort of a way. Like those pictures in kids' books of the good fairy in filmy white giving off an aura of light among the dark trees of the forest.

My eyes must have given me away. I don't know, maybe my mouth fell open.

She said, "You like it?"

I said something corny. But it was the first thing that popped into my head. "Would anyone like a million dollars? That's the way you look."

Her face would have illuminated the Grand Canyon. There was moisture glistening in her eyes and on her long lashes. Then I handed her the orchid. What a topper! She turned her back on me for a minute, crossed to the table and untied the ribbon. I knew she couldn't look at me right then without crying. Her eyes were still dewy when she turned back to me. She had the yellow orchid in her hand.

"Aren't you going to wear it?"

I saw her lips tremble slightly. She nodded and ran out of the room. A couple of seconds later she was back with the flower pinned on her shoulder.

Deb didn't talk on the way to the Spa. It was as if a spell had been cast over her and she didn't want to break it. We drove down the coast several miles and then took a blacktopped road that wound up through the hills. The fog we'd had for the past few nights had blown out to sea. Overhead the sky was spangled with bright stars. A half-moon rode low and unrolled a silver carpet over the restless dark water. The road climbed for a mile or so and came out on a tree-studded finger of land that pushed to the edge of the ocean.

Floodlights marked the small parking lot that had been carved out of the dense grove of giant eucalyptus trees. The lot was almost filled with big cars that gleamed expensively under the lights. My rented Pontiac looked like a poor relation. An attendant in a long, white linen coat took the car from the canopied doorway.

When my feet first sank into the deep-piled black carpet inside the door, I tried to figure the illusion. The dining room spread before us. It was light enough to see, and yet the room showed no evidence of lights. Then I got it. The room was semicircular. The walls from the ceiling to floor were sheets of glass. Outside, the eucalyptus grove was awash with floodlights.

The reflected light from the tannish trunks of the trees was enough to illumine the dining room. It gave a quiet restfulness to the place that was out of the world.

The headwaiter flashed Deb a smile. "You don't come here for a very long time."

I saw Deb wince. For a minute it made me hot. Why the hell did everybody have to keep rubbing the sore spot? I'd get her just where I wanted her, and then some dumb dodo like a headwaiter would have to throw a curve!

After we were seated at a table by the window the string orchestra started to play. The number was soft and dreamy. I could see it was getting her. She nodded for me to order for her.

The waiter brought the champagne.

We had both sipped part of a glass before she spoke. I knew by her eyes she was pulling the words out like they were too big for her throat. "You'll think I'm silly," she said, "but if it just weren't for these constant reminders …" Her voice faded away. Tears formed in her eyes.

I let a slow smile lift the corners of my mouth. My hand closed over hers. "I know, it's always like that…." I said it softly. "But you take it from there…."

She looked puzzled.

I said: "You see, everything is perspective…. When you came in here tonight the head waiter made a remark about your not having been here for a long time. It reminded you of the last time—the time you were with Jim. Then the orchestra played a piece—a piece Jim used to like. So you let it get you down…. I can't look at things like that…."

The orchestra started up again. Another soft dreamy tune with the violin carrying the melody.

Deb was looking at me like I was an oracle, a fountain of wisdom, and she was dying of thirst.

"I don't get what you mean," she said.

"Well, those memories that are making you so miserable—they're happy memories, aren't they?"

She nodded.

"Yet you're turning them into something else. Can't you let them give you some of the same happiness now they did when you were living them? Can't they enrich your life instead of embittering it?"

She wanted to cry. She was fishing around in her handbag for a handkerchief. I drew the one from my breast pocket and handed it to her. She daubed at her eyes and swallowed a lump in her throat.

I knew this was the place to turn it. To cut off the hearts and flowers and throw in the laughs. My timing was perfect!

"Women are all alike," I said. "Always mislaying things. Have I told you about my Aunt Phoebe in Philadelphia?" I smiled and lighted a cigarette. "The last time she started for Europe, she got to the railroad station and found her tickets weren't in her purse. She was frantic. She telephoned home and had her housekeeper turn the place upside down while she retired to the ladies' room and went through her fourteen petticoats. The tickets weren't to be found."

I laughed. "You should really hear Aunt Phoebe tell this part of it. She was standing on the station platform. The train was pulling out. It began to rain. She opened her umbrella—and the tickets showered out around her!"

Her laugh was weak but I got an encore. "Tell me more about Aunt Phoebe."

I refilled our champagne glasses and made up another string of lies. Her laughter grew stronger with each one. "You're very fond of her, aren't you, Rick?"

"She's a great old gal."

"I have several aunts but they're in the East. My mother died when I was born."

Her voice had dwindled and I was afraid for a minute she was swinging low again. But when I glanced up, her eyes were on me, soft and curious.

"Is your mother living?"

"No. She died before I was two."

"Do you remember her?"

Funny, I remembered her hardly at all, and yet there were scenes back in my mind, scenes as sharp as yesterday, her looking at me with her eyes soft and absorbed like Deb's eyes now. Crying. She was always crying. And one night, it must have been the night she died, me sitting on her bed alone in the room with her for a long time and her talking and talking, her eyes burning at me—and then her grabbing me and holding me and crying. I used to wake up at night for years after that seeing her eyes, trying to hear what she was saying....

"I know what she was saying."

Deb's voice brought me out of the fog with a bang. Christ! Was I blabbing all this to her?

Her hand was over mine now on the table. There was a path of tears down her cheeks but she was smiling.

"She was telling you all the things she wanted you to know," she said in a hushed voice, "—all the things she'd dreamed of telling you while you were growing up.... To be a good boy ... to remember her ... to take good care of your father...."

It was the damndest thing. I couldn't stop her. I felt as hollow as a balloon. I felt as if one of those soft words of hers could prick it and I'd collapse. But I couldn't stop her. I sat there like a drowning man, holding on to her hand as if it were the last solid thing in the world....

The movement must have caught my eye—a black arm lifting to summon a waiter. I didn't even know my glance had moved till it focused cold on the second table beyond ours.

Silky!

Everything turned red. But while I burned inside, I followed his movements. He didn't look once in our direction. But he'd seen us. He'd evidently finished his dinner. He must have been there for some time. The dirty earwigger. Spying on me. Taking in the scene at the table—our holding hands, our heads close together. He'd have someone waiting for me in the parking lot. To bring me to his place. To tell me she was ready for the play.

Treating me like a two-bit fink. Damn him!

We stayed until they played *Home, Sweet Home*, dancing every dance. I saw to it that Deb enjoyed herself. Because I wanted time to figure out an angle. To show Silky he couldn't call my part of the play.

It didn't do any good. When I said good-bye to her at her door, I knew it was for the last time. Tomorrow would come the frame, fast and smooth and relentless as Silky always pulled them.

She was telling me what a wonderful evening she'd had. "I *wish* you could have stayed a few more days." Her smile was wistful. She ran two fingers along my coat lapel.

"If wishes were horses." I grinned.

"You see Dad left for Frisco tonight. I'll be all alone—and I'm scared ..."

The words hit my brain, and my body went tense. "Your dad's gone?"

She was surprised at my vehemence. "Yes."

"How long is he going to be away?"

"About a week. It's something about park lighting...." Then she laughed. "I didn't mean to be a baby about it. Don't worry. I'll be all *right*...."

I wanted to grab her and kiss her. "You bet you'll be all right," I said. "I'll be here. I'll wire Aunt Phoebe in the morning."

I forgot all about the thirty-five-mile-an-hour speed limit on the way to Vista Del Mar. I wheeled into the crushed stone driveway and parked. Took the steps two at a time to the lobby and asked for Silky's suite. Going up in the elevator, I felt like a kid with a free ticket to the circus. So he'd try to push me around, would he? Well, I'd fix his wagon.

I rapped on his door. He yelled to come in.

He was sitting under a reading lamp by the window still in his dinner jacket. His smile was gentle, his voice oily.

"Looks like the Clark woman's ready for the play."

I tossed my hat on the table. I could afford enthusiasm. I said breezily, "Sure she's ready. When Fagan goes to work, things happen."

I could see his disappointment. He'd looked forward to putting on the screws. He said, "We'll pull the frame tomorrow night."

"Tomorrow night?" I flipped open his cigarette box and helped myself. "You mean a week from tomorrow night." I lit it and grinned through smoke at him. Grinned while his smugness slid off like last year's snakeskin and irritation tightened every muscle in his body.

"What's the joke?" he said.

I shrugged. "Her old man's gone to Frisco. We can't pull it without him."

When he could get his breath he began to curse.

## Chapter 10

The next morning while I was shaving it came to me. It was clear as a bell. I don't know what caused it. The human mind is a hell of a funny thing. It's like a stagnant pool with layers of the conscious on top, the subconscious below. During the night the subconscious had come to the top. I was through with Silky Angelo!

I didn't know how I was going to make the break. Right then I didn't give a damn. I knew I was. I was through with being pushed around. I was taking it from here. Then I thought about Dice. He was a good man. And doing a solo wasn't any good for the big con. I'd need a guy like him.

The approach, that was the thing that worried me. Dice was temperamental as an opera star. Sure, he was gambler from the word go, but then he liked the best of it. No sixty-to-one shots for that monkey. He liked to play the favorite straight across the board.

If the play was already in the oven, the excitement would bring him around. But cold turkey he didn't eat. I knew I'd get him okay but it would take some angling—but then, what the hell, angles were my specialty.

I finished shaving and dressed. I took my time. Savoring every minute of it. I was feeling swell. Eating my cake first. Saving the frosting till last. I picked a steel-grey homespun off the hanger. A number I'd had made in Asheville a couple of seasons ago. It was a swell-looking suit. Especially with the light-blue cashmere slipover that matched the color of my eyes. Carefully, I selected a necktie. A gay foulard, red and blue dots against a creamy-white background. I lighted a cigarette and strolled out into the hallway.

Downstairs, I thought of the little blonde filly in the doughnut shop. She liked my merry-go-round. Why not give her a ride?

The truckers and factory workers had eaten hours ago.

I thought at first the place was empty. I hoped so. Then I saw the greasy-haired kid that operated the switchboard at the Y.

He was huddled over a cup of coffee way at the back, talking to Beautiful. I knew he was sticky on her. He was laughing and looking up at her with eyes that all but sucked her in. She didn't seem to be minding it either. Not until she looked up and saw me. I took a stool about halfway back. The kid gave me a sickly look and nodded.

The filly brought me a glass of water. "Coffee?" she asked.

I nodded. She looked good enough to eat. She had on a thin yellow dress, a white fluffy apron. The neck was low, like before. Her yellow hair was twisted up on top of her head like fresh taffy. On some dames it would look silly. Like they were ready to take a bath. But on her it was perfect. She had eyes like Miriam Hopkins. The kind that danced when she talked.

"Doughnuts?" she asked.

"Sugar two," I said, lingering over the panoramic view.

She stood there absorbing it, pleased as a kitten, the neck of her dress going tight, then loose again. The kid down the way kept looking at me.

I heard him mumble something. I did a double take. He said it again. Something about a note in my box at the Y. Said a dame had been trying to get ahold of me on the telephone. Something important. At first I thought he was sore about me cutting him out with his girlfriend. Somehow, his eyes said he was playing it straight. I thought it must be Deb.

Beautiful trotted off and brought my coffee and sinkers. She set them down and started to linger. Just then a couple of customers dropped in. She pulled her eyes away from me and left. I drank up fast and polished off the doughnuts. She was still busy when I slipped a fifty-cent piece under my plate and went back to the Y.

Good old Charley was on the desk. He slobbered all over me before he handed me the note out of the box. On the way to the public phone booth I studied the number. It was one I'd never seen before. The thought flashed through my mind that it might be Tory. I'd warned her not to call. Maybe something had gone wrong.

I dropped my nickel in the slot and dialed. It was several minutes before anyone answered at the other end. When they did it was a strange girl's voice. Kind of low and cajoling. "Mr. Fagan?" it said. "You won't know me. I'm Joan Babcock, an old friend of Deb Clark's."

I said, "I'm glad to know you, Joan."

"Deb's told me about you. I think it's wonderful what you've done for her."

That was a hot one! I felt like saying I hadn't done much yet, but just give me time. Instead, I said, "I haven't done much."

She hesitated. Then said, "Debby's such a peach of a girl and we've all been so worried about her...."

"Yeah, I know."

She laughed shortly. "I called to ask you another favor. There's a dance tonight at the Surf and Saddle Club. I asked Deb a week ago and she turned me down. She hasn't felt like being with the old crowd since Jim's death. But we think she should come. It would do her good. And we think maybe if you asked her...."

For a minute I didn't know what to say. There might be a risk. Still the more solid I was with the town's elite, the more Owens would hesitate to expose me if the lid blew off. After all, a guy like that would think twice before he'd yell copper and have to admit his daughter had sponsored a con man with her choicest friends.

I said, "I agree with you. I can't make any promises, but I'll do my best."

She sounded pleased. "Call me back if you make the grade."

I said I would and hung up.

I called Deb. The maid answered. When Deb came to the phone I gave her the tale.

"I'm sorry, Rick," she said. "I'm afraid I just couldn't face the gang again ... right now ... maybe later...."

I let disappointment ooze into my voice. I sounded like a kid that found an empty stocking Christmas morning. "Sure, sure, I know how it is. I'll call the girl right back."

Deb said hastily, "But, Rick, you really want to go?"

I hesitated just long enough. Then I said, "No, forget it. At first I thought it did sound like fun. It's probably because I haven't been to a shindig like that since before the war. But I can wait another week. There'll be lots of them when I get back to Philly." I knew it was set. I had her pegged.

After a minute she said brightly, "You must go, Rick! I don't know what I was thinking of. I'll get you a darling girl...."

I broke this up fast. "Oh, no. If you won't go, I don't want to, Deb. Please. Let's forget it."

I could hear her quick intake of breath. After a minute she gave a wobbly laugh. "Well, I guess it wouldn't kill me."

I said: "I don't think you should force yourself. Of course, the Army still holds to the old rule of getting a man back in the air ten minutes after he crashes."

The pause was shorter this time. Her voice came back thin, almost gay. "All right, Rick. It's a date."

I said, "See here, I don't want you doing this on my account."

"Oh, no!" she lied brightly. "I want to go, Rick. Really I do. And it's lovely of you to take me."

I'd like to meet the guy who started the tale about men not understanding dames!

"I'll pick you up at eight," I said.

"Yes. And, Rick, you said you'd talk to Cotton Jennings, the boy who's taken over Jim's work? Advise him on equipment for the new building and everything. Could you make it this afternoon in his office?"

"I'll be looking forward to it," I told her. I would too. Like a guy looks forward to having a tooth pulled.

Joan Babcock was tickled silly. She called me a miracle man and said she'd drop the tickets off at the Y.

I hung up and swore under my breath. That was the hell of this racket. Always having to beat out a gum solo for some dope like Cotton Jennings. Sometimes I almost wished I had a sucker game—a restaurant, maybe, or a big storage garage....

I glanced at my watch. It was eleven-thirty. My rosy glow was shot. What I needed was a woman. I thought of Tory. I still had until one o'clock before I met Jennings. I thought again. Tory would be fatal. A few drinks, the afternoon would be shot before I knew what had happened. While I was walking out to the street I thought of the brown-haired dame in the real estate office.

The hot sun felt good on my head and shoulders. A teeming crowd jostled along the narrow sidewalk. Shop girls, stenos, shoe clerks hurrying out to catch a bite of lunch. I sauntered, leisurely taking in the shop windows, wondering what time the raggle put on the nosebag. Twelve seemed to be the rule in these jerky towns.

I turned a corner and ambled slowly past the real estate office. I saw her through the window, sitting at her desk. I knew she saw me. I didn't give her a tumble. Across the street was a pretty classy-looking eating joint called the Copper Room. I cut diagonally, dodging the noonday traffic, and went in.

A little bald-headed guy that had proprietor written all over him gave me a store-tooth grin and led me to a booth. I sat facing the street. Before he left, he shoved a menu into my hand.

I saw her come in. She hesitated a minute, looking around. I lowered my eyes like I was engrossed in the menu. She walked slowly over to the booth.

Without raising my eyes, I said, "You're late, New York."

I stood up and caught the look of surprise on her face. "What do you mean?" she demanded curtly.

"Sit down!"

As if the words had bowled her over, she let herself down slowly on the red leather seat across from me. I shook out a cigarette. Took my time blowing out the match. Then smiled at her.

"I gave you three minutes to put on your face and get over here after I walked by your office." I glanced at my wristwatch. "It's taken you four."

That made her hot. Her lips straightened into a hard line. She grabbed her purse, started to get up. "Well, of all the swell-headed, conceited punks...."

I was looking right at her. I started to pour honey fast. I said confidentially, "I shouldn't even be here. I cut a date to catch a few minutes with you. You're the best-looking gal I've seen in months. Ever since I met you the other day, I haven't been able to get you out of my mind."

Her feathers settled back into place. She sat down again. Looked interested. Picked up a stalk of celery and bit off a piece

savagely. Then smiled at me. "You devil."
I grinned. "I guess this wide spot in the road brings out the worst in me."
"You can say that again," she nodded agreeably. "If you ask me, Horace Greeley had a sense of humor like a rhinoceros."
"When do you leave for New York?"
She brightened. The word held magic for her. That's one of the secrets of handling skirts. Remember the details, the things they're interested in, and play them heavy.
The waiter came. I ordered for both of us. Started off with Martinis.
"I plan to leave in about a week," she said. "If I don't lose my mind before that." She sighed heavily. "This town has really got me down. If I stay out after ten my landlady acts like I've hit the primrose path. When are you shoving off?"
"About a week."
She brightened again. Slipped a card from her purse. "Here's my New York address just in case you hit town and can't do better."
I patted her hand. "You mean they do come better?"
She just smiled at me. "You're nice."
The waiter brought the cocktails. We sipped them and talked a lot of nonsense. Then ate lunch. I was surprised when I looked at my watch. It was ten minutes of one.
Getting up, I said, "I've got to run. Got an appointment with some dope in the City Building."
She opened her purse and started digging. I slipped three singles from my wallet and folded them over the check.
"I'm paying my own," she protested mildly, fishing out some money.
"Not when you eat with me," I said.
She laughed. "Maybe you haven't heard. This is the West where men are men, and women pay their own checks."
"I don't hear well," I said. "Anyway, I'm from Philly, remember?"
I promised to try and call her some night if I could break away. She was glowing like a red-hot stove when she said good bye.
Going up to the third floor in the City Building, I realized I felt

better. Even equal to this Cotton Jennings ordeal. The gal from the real estate office had put me back on the trolley again.

I stepped off the elevator, went down a light, airy hall until I found his name inscribed in block letters on a frosted-glass door.

To my knock he called a friendly "Come in." He was obviously waiting for me. Sitting behind a metal desk with a plate glass top.

Noiselessly he pushed back his chair and got to his feet. He threw a hand at me that looked like a Swift's Premium. Jennings was one of the first men I'd met in a long time I didn't have to look down to. He was six feet two and must have tilted the scales at two and a quarter. Strictly the football type. No neck at all, and shoulders like the Blue Ridge Mountains. His smile wasn't confined to his mouth, but extended in a ruddy glow over his square face.

He practically engulfed me in a gush of joy and appreciation over my finding time to drop in and see him. While he jabbered on about what a fine girl Deb Clark was, I took a gander around the office. He had the maps Deb had described to me thumbtacked all over one wall with dozens of colored pins showing the redder or bluer districts. On the wall opposite was a large portrait of Knute Rockne; beside it, a picture of Jim Clark.

Underneath was a redwood case with a glass panel in front. It was full of medals. He saw me looking at it. He seemed pleased.

He opened it and began dragging out the medals. "These probably look plenty familiar to you," he grinned. "I'll bet you were with Jim when most of these were won."

It was a broadside. I didn't dare look at him: I said, "We were on a lot of missions together." I turned one of the medals over in my hand. On the back was inscribed Jim's initials, J.D.C., and the date the medal was presented.

Jennings saw me looking at an empty hook in the case. Beneath it was a small, typed card reading: "Sharpshooter Medal, Jan. 5, 1942."

He shook his head. "That one was lost in the mails while Jim was still in the States. It made Deb about sick, although it's the least important of them all."

"Sure," I agreed. "Practically all of us came home with those."

"Right after Jim was killed," Jennings said, "Deb insisted we keep his medals up here for the kids to see. Things like these are a wonderful influence on the juvenile mind. And they worshipped Jim Clark."

I nodded enthusiastically. I looked as if I was hanging on every word.

He closed the redwood case almost reverently and went back to his desk. He sat down and nodded me into a chair directly across from him. He said: "Deb told me you'd have a lot of ideas on the new plant we're setting up. On the way we're working on the juvenile delinquency problem."

I had my guard up. Sure I had ideas on their work, and what a shock they'd be to him! But I didn't have to worry about handing out the gab this time. He was bursting for the chance to let off some of his enthusiasm. All I had to do was toss the ball back to him and he'd make the play.

I said: "I'm only an amateur at boys' work. I've always been interested, but never really made a study of it. Jim was kind of pioneering, wasn't he?"

He was off to the races. For the next hour, his mouth never stopped. He gave me a full-length feature of this Jerk-town Jove in action. Of his industry, his patience, his accomplishments.

When he couldn't think of any more about Hart City, he told me about "Teen Town," a movement in New Orleans, near the old French Quarter, that had given Jim a lot more notions.

It had been started by some psalm-singing monkey to keep the kids from getting sneezed. He told how the place was equipped with a snack bar, lending library, swing band. How they had art classes, movies and lectures to direct their thinking along proper lines.

I wondered what he thought was proper. Making a crop of suckers out of kids that might really go places with the wire or the rag.

He told how the kids really ran the joint. How they elected a kid mayor, all the city officials, held their own courts.

When I thought he was almost run down, he got going again.

About how war had increased juvenile delinquency because of mothers away from home working in war plants and kids having too much money. Of the kids' watchword: "Have fun today for tomorrow we may die."

What the hell, I thought, was the matter with that?

By now I was so jittery I couldn't sit still in my chair. I lighted a cigarette. Tried to hold an absorbed expression on my pan.

Then all of a sudden Jennings said something that rang a bell.

"I don't care which place Deb buys for the boys but I kind of favor Seaview Villa. That woods, and that clubhouse. They'd be fine, wouldn't they? There's something about that place that gets me."

"Yes, there is," I said. The bell went on ringing. An idea was there if I could get hold of it!

"Of course, a hundred thousand is a lot of money to pay for a boys' club."

While I was nodding, it hit me. He went on talking but I didn't hear him. That idea had crashed through. And what an idea! It was a play the Yellow Kid had pulled once on a real estate deal on a home for the blind. Christ! It was made to order for the setup here! That hundred thousand dollars was right in my hand.

I was as good as free of Silky!

I tried to cover my excitement. As soon as I could, I told Jennings I had to meet a man at three. I shook his hand and got out of his office.

While the elevator went down, my spirits were soaring up—and fast.

## Chapter 11

For the next two hours I was like a guy walking in his sleep. I don't know where all I went. I know my legs just kept carrying me along. It was as if my mind didn't have any connection with my body. I remember going down to the ocean. Dragging my feet through the warm, soft sand. Walking, walking, walking. My mind going over a thousand different angles of how I could pull the play. It was bound to be risky. Christ, if Silky ever got wise....

I guess my mind finally wore itself out. I was back in town walking along the same street the Y was on when I noticed a clock in a jeweler's window. It was ten minutes after five. I had to go back to my room and get ready for the shindig.

Two blocks down the street I stopped in a florist's shop. I bought a shoulder spray of camellias. While I was waiting for my change I noticed a placard advertising the dance. So it was a benefit! That little item Deb's girlfriend forgot to mention. And it might be important to the play I'd partly worked out in my mind. Swell chance to put on a show for the customers. Quickly I thumbed through the bills in my wallet—fifty-seven bucks. Chicken feed! I thought of Silky. Maybe I could put the arm on him. I glanced at my watch. It was five-thirty. Too late to drive to the Vista Del Mar.

I thought of the roll I had stashed in the Cadillac. It seemed a shame to use my own sugar even if it was my show. The man came with the box of flowers and my change. I beat it out the door.

At the storage garage I told the punk I had to get something out of my car. He tossed me the keys and went back to figuring on his books. It was dark in the back of the low building where my car was parked. I raised the turtleback, found my secret compartment and fished out my roll. I peeled off five C notes and buried it again. Just to be sure, I gave the starter a whirl. The battery was still up in good shape. When I came back to the office I stuck my head in and yelled at the kid.

"Have that crate ready to roll in the morning. Check the

tires, change the oil and fill 'er with gas—ethyl."

He asked me what time I was going to need it. I felt like cracking I'd need it as soon as I parted a dumb widow from her bank roll. Instead, I said, "Have it ready by nine, sure."

He said he would and grinned when I tossed him a shiny half dollar.

In my racket it doesn't pay to take any chances with the getaway car. You never know when you're going to have to cop a heel. I wanted things set—just in case.

I caught a sandwich and a cup of Java in a corner drugstore on the way back to the Y. I wanted plenty of time to get into the glad rags.

I let the hot shower splash over me for a long time, shaved carefully and started to dress. The white dinner jacket pointed up my bronzed face. The salt air put just the right amount of wave in my hair. I was in the pink. No doubt about that. I don't know why, but for a minute I thought about getting old. Wrinkles all over my puss, a paunch to spoil the drape of my clothes. Then I grinned at myself. Hell, why think about that! By the time I'm old I'll have so much dough stashed away, looks won't matter....

I drove out and picked up Deb. She thanked me for the flowers and then clammed up all the way to the dance. It was a perfect night. A full moon rode high in the sky, and spidery wisps of clouds dragged like streamers over its silver face. The ocean was almost glassy and a soft gentle wind poured in the open car windows. I felt romantic.

We parked across the highway from the temporary pavilion the club had built on the sand. There were cars everywhere and people streaming in. The soft rhythm of an expensive dance band floated in the air. The dance floor was built up on the pilings. Around the sides were papier-mâché palm trees that were too green and rattled in the slightest breeze. Colored lanterns hung everywhere and cast a soft aura of light over the dancers. At one end was a huge bandshell painted silver with blue spots moving back and forth.

As we came up the ramp the band stopped playing. Then a loud crash of cymbals and a long roll on the drums. Through the crowd I saw a guy emerge from a group of dolls. They'd been huddled together like players at a football game. Each had a silver plate in her hand to take up the benefit collection.

We stopped at the edge of the dance floor and I grinned down at Deb. I said, "Wouldn't you know we'd get here just in time for the collection? My luck always did run like that. When I was a kid I used to walk into the church just in time to catch the offertory."

She laughed more than the crack warranted and I sensed it was nerves.

A cute little redhead in a green evening dress breezed up to us. She spoke to Deb, then turned her eyes to me. She held the plate in her hand. I pulled out my wallet and fingered the five century notes. Casually I pulled them out and let them flutter onto the plate. Deb's eyes widened as she looked up at me. The kid in the green let out a squeal and disappeared into the crowd. Before Deb had recovered her voice she was back again, dragging another girl with her. The new number had a pencil and notebook in her hand.

Breathlessly she said, "I'm Mary Innis from the *Gazette*. We're publishing a list of the largest donors in tomorrow's night edition. Looks like your name will head the list."

I put on my modest look. Said confidentially, "If you don't mind, I'd rather keep it anonymous. I'm superstitious about donor lists."

They both thanked me profusely and went away jabbering between themselves.

The music started up again. I looked down at Deb. The color had drained from her face. She swayed against me. "What's the matter?" I asked.

She dropped her eyes. "I ... I ... don't know," she stammered. "Too much excitement for me, I guess." She forced a shaky laugh.

I took her arm and steered her toward the clubhouse. "What you need is a drink."

The room was in semidarkness. The only light flooded the mirrors on the back bar and struck pin points of light from rows of polished glasses. The bar itself was in the shape of a horseshoe. Made of slabs of black glass. The bar stools were miniature saddles of white shiny leather. We slid onto them and I ordered Martinis for both of us.

Deb sipped hers slowly and kept looking at me from the corner of her eyes. Finally in a low voice she said, "I hope you didn't give all that money tonight because you thought I'd expect you to."

I laughed. "Plenty more where that came from. You see my aunt, the one I told you about in Philly, set up a large trust fund for me when I was born. The interest now amounts to more than I can ever spend."

"Oh, I see." She said it thoughtfully.

She went back to her drink. I just sat there rolling the slender stem of my glass between two fingers. A nostalgic feeling kept bothering me. You know how it is. As though I'd been in that same place before, saying the same words, listening to the same music drift in through the windows. After a while Deb said, "I guess we're both feeling quiet tonight."

I told her how it was. The strange feeling I had. Only the way it seemed to me, it was Miami instead of Hart City. I decided it was just because of the looks of the bar. It was like a lot of them along Collins on the beach. That and the same heavy pounding of the surf outside, the throbbing strains of the dance music.

Couples started drifting in from the dance. Several, including the dame that sold me the tickets, stopped to say hello to Deb. Each time I could see her whole body tighten. It was an ordeal for her. She introduced me with a certain pride she couldn't keep out of her voice.

I ordered another round of drinks. More people stopped by. Some of the dolls were very special. Most of them gave me the eye. God, I thought, if I were only on the loose. Oh well, it's like the old hunter said, "The things a guy sees when he doesn't have a gun!"

The music started again. The bar began to empty. I asked Deb if she wanted to dance. She didn't seem too enthusiastic, but she said she would. We surged up the ramp with the others and onto the floor. It was so crowded you couldn't really dance. Just sort of walk around trying to miss other couples. It was about halfway through the dance that it happened. We were at the far end of the pavilion, right near the bandshell. Deb had her face partly buried in my shoulder. Suddenly she looked up at me. "That man," she said. "The singer. He's been trying to wave at you."

I took a quick look, and turned my head away fast. It was Eddie Lukins, a loud-mouthed crooner, who'd warbled with the band at the Hollywood Beach Hotel in Miami last season.

As fast as I could, I steered Deb for the other end of the floor. My back was ringing wet. I could feel the clamminess of my shirt sticking to me.

"Why didn't you speak to him?" Deb demanded.

"He wasn't waving at me," I said. "He waved and then called a name. I think it was Maxon."

I didn't think a thing about it. I knew goddamned well he called Maxon. That was the phony monicker I was using at the time I knew him. It would be just swell if he breezed up to us and started reminiscing about Miami! I knew right then I had to get out of there. I didn't know how, but I'd figure something.

That's the thing that makes con men wake up screaming. People always showing who knew you from another job.

It explained one thing—that familiar feeling I'd been having. It was this monkey's voice that made it seem I'd been here before. Christ a'mighty, I'd had to listen to him for fourteen nights while I tied up a visiting sucker.

When the music stopped, I suggested we take a walk along the beach. Deb went for it like a tarpon taking the bait. We went down the ramp and walked along the hard-packed sand where the ocean had pounded it smooth. There was a queer greenish glow to the waves I'd never seen before. It was as if each wave had a neon tube strung along the crest. The green reflected down into the curve of the wave. We stopped to look at it.

"What kind of a lighting system do you use in your ocean out here?" I asked.

Deb laughed. "That's phosphorus. It only happens once in a while."

"It's beautiful," I said.

"Isn't it though. When I was a kid I used to always swim on

nights when the phosphorus came in. I'd imagine I was living in another world. A world all my own where no one else could enter."

"You must have been an imaginative kid," I said. "I guess I always was too."

I took hold of her hand and we strolled slowly along in the moonlight.

Suddenly she stopped. Looked up at me. Her eyes were pleading. "Let's swim tonight. We can get suits at the club."

"You mean you'll let me in on that little private world of yours?"

She nodded and winked tears away that had sprung into her eyes.

If I didn't get the breaks! The last thing in the world I wanted to do was plunge into that black, cold water. There was an angle to it, at that. I wouldn't run into that punchy crooner in there.

We went back to the club. Deb led the way around to a door that opened onto the beach. There was a cement stairway that led down to the locker room. A sleepy-looking kid was on duty. He found suits to fit us. By the time I had slid into the trunks he gave me, my teeth were beating out a rumba. I looked in a mirror. My lips were blue.

Outside again it seemed warmer than the damp chill of the basement. I walked up and down waiting for Deb. Trying to get my blood moving. I heard the door when it opened. I turned and there she stood. She had on a white suit that molded her perfect figure. Her hair was loose and fell across smooth white shoulders. The moonlight washed down over her. She was more beautiful than I'd ever seen her.

Her eyes took me in. Measured the width of my shoulders, slid down to my narrow waist.

"Atlas," she said and laughed. "I'll race you to the raft."

She pounded away through the sand and plunged into the water. I was only a step behind her. The cold water hit me and snatched my breath away. I gulped a few times and found it again.

She was cutting through the water like the blade of a knife. Long powerful strokes with barely a ripple. I clenched my teeth hard and gave it all I had. Pains shot through my legs. My lungs felt like bursting. Ahead the black outlines of the float rolled with the surf. Twice I thought I'd have to give up and quit. Then I'd remember the role I was playing. The returned soldier. Seasoned and tough from the rigors of battle. I pushed myself to the limit. Passed Deb twenty yards from the goal. Finally my fingers struck the canvas that edged the diving float. The strength was all drained out of me. I was panting heavily. My mouth was cotton. I struggled up the ladder and pulled Deb up after me.

She was winded, too, but not like me. We both lay back resting. Overhead the blue-black sky was filled with stars, the moon dropping a silver veil over a world of blackness. The soft, gentle breeze poured over us. With a contented sound the small swells lapped salty tongues against the restless diving raft. The muted throbbing of dance music rose and softened with the offshore wind.

Deb turned her head and faced me. Tiny glistening drops of water shone against the whiteness of her skin. Quietly she said, "You certainly cut a swath tonight. I saw every woman in the place looking at you." I could feel a hurt in her tone. She was jealous!

"They always look at strangers," I muttered. "You know, they're like curios in small towns. Something new and different."

She laughed shakily. "I wonder."

I wanted to change the subject. I said, "You did a swell job of meeting all your old friends. I feel a lot better now about leaving."

I could see her stiffen. "You're not going—right away?" she said tightly.

"I promised Aunt Phoebe."

"You said when the memorial business was settled."

"We can settle it tonight."

"Yes," she said like it hurt. "Yes, we could decide tonight. I'm just being selfish."

I didn't answer. My hand found hers and pressed it. We lay there a long time listening to the waves ... looking up at the stars ... not talking.

Then she said, "How do you really feel about all the places we've seen?"

I grinned. "Don't ask me tonight. I feel expansive ... and expensive."

"You mean Seaview Villa is your choice?"

"Uh huh."

"Mine too," she said.

"That's the one your friend Cotton Jennings likes. He told me so today. He hated to mention it to you because of the cost."

She didn't answer, but in the pale light I could almost see her making up her mind.

She turned and looked at me. Her eyes were shining as if they'd collected some of that phosphorus out there in the surf.

"An idea came to me," she said softly, "tonight when you gave that five hundred dollars to the charity fund."

I raised on one elbow and looked at her.

Her smile was uncertain. "I know what conclusion the town will come to when the memorial is given anonymously too."

"They'll think I gave it?"

"Do you mind?"

"Why should I? I'll be on the other side of the continent. If it'll make it easier for you, it's okay with me."

I felt an increased pressure of her hand. She turned her head away. I was glad she did. My brain was starting to sizzle. I'd thought out a couple of new steps in the play. The time had come for me to really go to work.

I lay there going over the buildup. It seemed tight. I took the plunge.

"Honey."

She turned her head to me.

"There's something I've been wanting to ask you for several days now—I've been afraid to. If you think I'm out of order, just say so."

Her eyes widened. "I will."

I let the words stumble out of me. "Well, you see I thought an awful lot of Jim, too. Probably more than I'll ever think of any other man again. I told you tonight I had a lot of money. More than I'll ever need. I'd like to pay for half of that memorial."

I heard the quick intake of her breath. She snapped her head away from me. Then started to cry. I stroked her hair.

I said quickly, "Never mind. Just forget I said it. I had a nerve butting in."

Her sobbing stopped. Brokenly she said, "No, it isn't that, Rick, how could I be angry about that? It's just that ... well ... it's so wonderful to think that you really cared that much for Jim. Of course you can pay for half."

"I really want to be in on it," I said. And that was no lie.

I didn't want to ham it up, but I was so excited inside it was hell just lying there waiting until I thought I could tactfully suggest we go.

Finally she gave me the break. She said something about getting cold. We swam back to shore leisurely, dressed and I took her home.

I left her at her door, promising I'd phone in the morning. I drove like hell back to town. I knew an all-night beanery where they had a telephone booth. I parked the boiler and went in. My hands were shaking so I could hardly get the damn nickel in the telephone slot. I dialed a number and waited. Then I heard the brunette's voice. The one from the real estate office. She sounded hazy from sleep.

I said, "New York?"

She giggled.

"Get into a dress," I snapped. "We're going for a moonlight ride."

## Chapter 12

I picked up New York in front of her boarding house ten minutes later. She got in fast with a nervous laugh.

"God, these small towns!" She looked back as we drove off. "One of these days I'll be laughing at little things."

"The landlady?"

"Uh huh. She was breathing down my neck at the phone." Her eyes took on an extra sparkle as she looked at me, taking in my white dinner jacket. "Listen, I didn't dress...."

"Baby, you don't need to."

She giggled. "I had to tell her it was Mr. McNulty and business. You'll have to give me a good story when I go back."

I put my arm around her and pulled her up close. "It *is* business, Beautiful," I said.

"Yeah?" she murmured happily. "What kind?"

"Deb Clark has taken a notion she wants to see Seaview Villa in the moonlight."

She pulled back to look at me, puzzled. "You kidding?"

"No."

"What's that got to do with me?"

"Thought I could kill two birds with one stone—get the key from your office and give you a quick ride at the same time."

She let out a sound like air rushing from an inner tube. After a minute she said, "Oh." She sounded mad. "So, I'm just a convenience."

I looked at her and put on the brake. I said coldly, "Sorry. I can get the key from McNulty."

She caught the wheel when I started to make a U-turn. "Don't be so touchy," she grinned. "I'm at your mercy. A quick ride's better than none."

I tucked her hand under mine on the steering wheel. "All depends on who you're with."

She moved closer.

A salt fog was blowing in from the ocean. The street lights blinked through it dismally, marking off deserted streets.

McNulty's was dark as a tomb.

New York opened the front door with a key from her purse and we felt our way in. "Better not turn on the lights," she whispered, "or the whole town will be over asking questions."

This suited me fine. We bumped our way across the outer office, New York giggling with the excitement of it. At the keyboard I lit matches while she went through the tags to find the Seaview Villa key.

It took three matches. She was trying to drag it out. But finally she found the key. I blew out the last match just as it started to burn my finger.

And then we heard the rattling at the door!

It was a bad minute. New York clutched my arm, and we held our breaths. It could be the night watchman, of course. But again, it could be McNulty coming down for a spot of night work. I'd have a sweet time explaining this nocturnal yen of Deb Clark's. And he might insist on going along.

The door opened. A powerful flashlight plowed through the darkness, picked us out. A man's voice said, "Oh! Miss Kramer."

New York let out her breath on a laugh. "It's the merchant police."

I said, "We were getting a key and didn't turn on the lights just to save you the trouble of investigating us."

He took it as a good joke. He was relieved, too, it hadn't been someone to make him trouble. He sat on the edge of New York's desk and smoked a cigarette, and told us how lonesome the town was at night.

The incident served a good purpose. New York had had her thrill. She felt repaid for dressing and coming out and was content to let me drive her straight back to her boarding house. She said it was the most exciting night she'd had since she'd been here.

I said, "Wait till we get back to the Big City. We'll make up for lost time," I drew her up against me. "At the risk of this being an anticlimax...." I kissed her hard. I could feel the surprised tremor go through her, then she relaxed and enjoyed it.

Before she could get her breath, let alone ask for more, I hustled her out of the car and up the steps of the old frame building.

I said, "Better not mention our little key-lifting to McNulty, Beautiful. No use getting yourself in wrong. I'll be in in the morning and tell him all about it."

"Okay," she said. She was still breathless. "Thanks."

I could see the shadow of the landlady on the blind as I went down the steps. This was a break. She'd keep New York busy explaining so she wouldn't try thinking things out.

I drove straight to Dice's hotel. The lobby was deserted, except for the night clerk. I went up to the desk and asked if Mr. Gentry was in.

The clerk roused out of his sleepy stupor. He scratched his bald head just above his ear with the eraser of his pencil, and muttered that he was in and he'd call. What was my name?

"Never mind," I said genially. "I don't need an introduction." I stepped into the self-service elevator. Before the doors clanged shut, I had a glimpse of the fat little guy swinging hastily around to the switchboard. I grinned.

The corridor of Dice's floor reeked of cigar smoke. I strode silently up to his door and listened a minute. There was a lot of to-do inside ... tiptoeing feet ... scraping noises.

My knock brought Dice, trying to cover his nervousness with a stagy yawn. I laughed and gave him a poke in the midriff. He let out a bellow of rage. "You!" he said, disgusted.

I pushed past him into the smoky room. "Some night," I murmured, "it *will* be Silky."

Dice shut the door and came back in. "Some night you and your jokes are getting a load of lead in the belly," he said.

He rattled slightly when he walked. "Did you swallow your winnings?" I asked him.

Sulkily he dumped onto the table a handful of chips he had scraped into his pocket. "Ten to one," he griped, "they won't come back. They were plenty burned about getting the bum's rush."

"And down the service elevator."

"Yeah." He sighed. "It was such a nice bunch of suckers, too, damn you. That stove salesman from Peoria had his last year's commission check on him."

I lit a cigarette and grinned at him. "You won't have time for subway dealing when you come in with me," I said.

He snarled. "Who the hell says I'm coming in with you?"

"Nobody. I'm giving you a chance, that's all."

He snapped those brilliant suspenders of his till he winced at their sting. He said, "Why you conceited bastard, I wouldn't come in with you if you were the last grifter on earth, see? Not even if you were as good as you think you are."

I went on smiling, watching him. I shrugged. "Okay," I said. "I just came up to give you first chance. I flipped a coin and it came up you. Since you don't want it, I'll pick up Max Graber."

Dice sneered. "Think you're going to start a play on your own, eh?"

"I have started it," I said quietly. I got up.

"So, it's the tear-off, eh?"

"Silky and I are dissolving partnership."

"What makes you think he'll stand around and take it?"

"Nobody's standing around. Tomorrow morning at nine-thirty, I'm blowing this burg with a hundred grand."

Dice was sweating the way he always did when he got on dead center. The guy had no vision. But he was a smooth operator when you spelled it out for him. I needed him worse than I'd admit tonight.

"This is like you," he said bitterly. "Giving a guy no chance to figure things out...."

"It's a simple problem," I said. "Just a matter of whether you want to put your money on Silky or me. I don't want to influence you one way or the other."

"Silky's been an inside man a hell of a lot longer than you have."

"That's right. Of course, if you came in with me, you'd be getting in on the ground floor. You'd be my first roper."

"Yeah, but I'm not so sure you could play 'em when I got 'em for you."

"Fine," I said cheerfully, "I'll see if Max has more confidence in me. Sorry I couldn't give you more time, Dice, but things are moving too fast tonight." I started out this time. I figured I'd turned up my trump. Dice never could resist the excitement of the play.

For a minute I thought I'd lost. I was at the door before he made a sound. My fingers froze around the knob at his cough. He said, "Crissake, can't you let me get my hat?"

I helped him pack. Then I drove him to the Y, explaining the play on the way. He had to admit it was smooth.

We went up to my room and he put in the call to Deb while I changed into slacks and a sport coat.

Deb herself answered the phone. Probably she was the only one up.

Dice said, affable and apologetic, "Mrs. Clark? Oh, fine! This is Joe Swanson from the McNulty Realty Company." There was a questioning buzz.

Dice said, "No, you don't know me, Mrs. Clark. I haven't had the pleasure of working on your deal. But Mr. McNulty is away on business tonight and an emergency has come up. I tried to get you at the Club, but you'd left."

Another buzz of explanation, upending in a question. Dice said, "Well, it's like this, Mrs. Clark. An out-of-town client, who's been considering Seaview Villa, dropped into the office tonight and wanted to close the deal. I looked it up and found it listed among the places Mr. McNulty had shown you. I was in a bit of a quandary, because I know Mr. McNulty is anxious for you to get the place you want. At the same time I couldn't turn down a sale of this magnitude."

I could catch the overtone of concern in the buzz this time, and I felt better.

Dice said, "No, I didn't sell it, Mrs. Clark. I asked him to wait. I told him I'd have to contact Mr. McNulty because I believed he had taken a check on the place. However, there's a bad catch to it. Mr. McNulty won't be home till late tomorrow. And this client says he'll wait only until nine-thirty in the morning. He wants to make the ten-o'clock train."

Dice was doing it well. He sounded like a young salesman jittery over his first big deal. He kept repeating how he hated to bother her and how he certainly didn't want her to feel he was trying any high-pressure salesmanship on her. It was just that this deal had come up in Mr. McNulty's absence and he wanted to do the best for everyone concerned.

He lowered his voice and said, "I understand, of course, that this deal of yours is strictly on the q.t., so naturally I didn't mention your name. I thought possibly you might have made up your mind by now that you weren't interested in Seaview Villa...."

He winked at me as Deb's voice broke in. His thumb-and-forefinger circle assured me she was very much interested in Seaview Villa.

"Well then," he said, and his voice quavered with nervousness, "I'll just have to see if I can get in touch with Mr. McNulty."

I knew what Deb was saying without leaning forward. She was hating to put him on such a spot. And he shouldn't wire Mr. McNulty just yet. Maybe she could make up her mind before morning. She'd try to make up her mind tonight.

Dice said, "Well that's sure nice of you, Mrs. Clark. Say, maybe you'd like to go out and see the place once more. I could drop by the office and pick up a key...."

He hung up soon after that, grinning. "That baby is made to trim," he said.

I tossed him a white shirt of mine, and while he exchanged it for the raspberry number he'd been wearing, I wrote a quick note on plain paper, notifying Charley I'd been called out of town on business. I enclosed money to settle my bill at the Y and prepay express on my bags to Tulsa, Oklahoma. (Tulsa, I figured, was one town I'd never have reason to visit.) I thanked him kindly for his trouble and assured him of the pleasant and profitable visit I'd had at the Y.M.C.A. This would be no lie. I wasn't the kind of operator who left loose ends—who'd spoil the play for a twenty-dollar room bill. And I figured if my name stayed good in the town, it was a fifty-to-one shot Deb and her father would take the hundred-grand loss rather than let themselves in for notoriety that might spell political ruin to him and a nervous breakdown to her.

The phone rang while I was folding my letter. I let it ring while I stamped the envelope and addressed it. I slipped it into my pocket as I picked up the receiver. I'd mail it just as we left Hart City tomorrow morning.

I remember to sound hoarse from sleep. "Hello."

Deb was excited. She told me the real estate company had just called. We had only until nine-thirty tomorrow morning if we wanted to buy Seaview Villa.

I fumbled around foggily. "What's this? Nine-thirty? What's wrong? Why should we buy it by nine-thirty?"

She explained fast. She said she'd arranged to go out and see the place again tonight. "Rick," she said, "would it be an awful imposition for me to ask you to go along?"

"It would have been a hell of a thing if you hadn't," I said.

She gave a little laugh of relief. She said Mr. Swanson was coming by for her. Then she gasped, "I forgot to tell him to pick you up. I'll call him right back. I can catch him at the office ..."

"I'll call him," I said fast. "I can dress quicker than you can." I hung up, grinning. "You got me in a squeeze play that time," I told Dice, "but I made it."

Then minutes later Dice and I picked Deb up and we drove out to the estate.

Deb said softly, "How do you feel about it?"

Her voice gave her away. She was in love with this place, with the feeling of peace and warmth it gave her. The vision of it just now in the moonlight—its sweep of lawns, the symmetry of silvered masses of walls and roofs, echoed this beauty.

She was unaware of any connection between this attachment of hers for Seaview Villa and the hour I had held her hand here in this garden and her senses had swung from their stultified absorption in the dead past to the realm of the living. Not knowing it was her emotion dictating her choice, she couldn't even distrust it. She was putty.

I pressed her hand. I whispered, "How do you feel about it?"

"I think it's our place."

Her eyes lifted, smiled anxiously into mine.

I nodded. "I've thought so all along."

It came to me then how unerring my instinct had been. When we looked at this place, I hadn't the play in mind, no reason for believing it mattered to me whether she chose the big place or one of the inexpensive estates. But it was in this garden I had made love to her. That's the kind of grifter sense you can't buy.

Hand in hand we wandered back across the lawns to the house. Dice was waiting for us on the loggia. I hoped she wouldn't notice the formidable mound of cigarette stubs beside him. But his voice held only friendly concern.

"Don't let me rush you, Mrs. Clark. Take all the time you need."

Deb's radiant glow dimmed the moonlight patina. She said, "We want the house, Mr. Swanson."

"You do!"

There was a definite crack of relief in his voice. I covered fast. I said, "It was decent of you, Mr. Swanson, to give us this last chance at it." I gave him a look.

Dice got control of himself. "Not at all," he said briskly. "We have a reputation for integrity at McNulty's. If I didn't uphold that reputation, I wouldn't work there very long."

"I feel sorry for that client," Deb said. "And this will mean you'll only make one sale instead of two."

"Never mind about that," Dice cried genially. "You know the old saying. There's a su—client born every minute. And there's only one California coastline. We'd like to have a dozen more of these estates."

There was nothing slow about Dice once he got started.

We walked back through the house, Dice pottering along behind us, closing doors and making general noises like a real estate punk.

I decided it was time to bring the play to a head. I said to Dice: "It'll be a cash deal." I turned to Deb. "That's right, isn't it?"

"Of course. Any way you think best."

"Cash is always best for the buyer," Dice said.

"I'm going halves with Mrs. Clark on the deal," I told him. "I'll wire my bank when we get back to town and they can rush back a draft in the morning."

Dice said, "Uh huh," and tried the catch on a door. "Where is your bank, Mr. Fagan?"

"Philadelphia."

"Uh *huh*." His voice climbed up through a dark well of worry.

"What's wrong?" Deb asked.

"Nothing—nothing, ordinarily," Dice muttered. "Let's see now.

Your wire would be on the desk of your bank when they opened tomorrow morning. They'd wire us the money. But even if they did it promptly, and if there were no tie-ups at the telegraph office...."

"You mean it wouldn't be here by nine-thirty?" I said.

He shrugged. "I don't see how it could, except through a miracle, do you?"

I said impatiently, "But you *know* we're buying. What's a delay of fifteen or twenty minutes?"

Dice looked unhappy. "If only Mr. McNulty were here," he mourned. "He'd know of a way to handle this client. You see, I told the guy this check was in. He acted a little huffy at the time, like he thought I was trying to put one over on him. I wouldn't be at all surprised if he demanded to see the check tomorrow morning. And if I don't have it, I don't know how I can hold him off."

"He'll have to take your word for it," I said irritably. "I haven't the money on me. I couldn't carry it in my sock overseas."

Deb was breathing fast from the effort to follow the conversation. She broke in excitedly, "But look, why can't I write you a check for the full amount, Mr. Swanson? That would make us safe, wouldn't it?"

"Well—yes. Sure." Dice frowned at her. "If you want to do it that way."

I began a violent protest. "But I'm buying half ..."

"He can pay me, can't he?" Deb pleaded with Dice. "Can't you write up the deed to both of us and then he can settle with me?"

"Oh, sure," Dice said.

"Well, then!" She beamed at me dewily, proud of her business acumen. The little dope. The cute little sucker.

I said, "Well, thank goodness there's one business brain here."

She laughed. There is nothing that goes to a dame's head like believing she's outsmarted a man at his own game. "Just make the check out to the McNulty Real Estate Office," Dice instructed. "No, wait...." His voice labored under heavy concern. "Mr. McNulty said you wanted this deal kept strictly on the q.t. That right?"

"Yes," Deb said.

"Then that check going through our office wouldn't be so good."

He was coming now to the weak spot in our play. We were taking a chance and we knew it. The play could go one of two ways—and the second way was plenty risky.

Deb was watching him anxiously.

He said slowly: "I'm afraid it's going to be a lot of bother for you, Mrs. Clark. But I don't know any other way of doing it. I'll run up to your house tomorrow at eight-thirty and you give me a check for cash. I'll have it down at the office at nine when this client comes in. Then as soon as he's gone, I'll call you and you come down to the bank. I'll have the contracts drawn up. We can turn them and the cash over to the escrow department."

I said, "I'll come and get you, Deb. I can at least do the running around since I can't swing my end of the deal." I sounded forlorn. I sounded like a man who's sensitive about a woman taking the reins.

I could feel Deb looking at me, could almost feel the fevered glow of her excitement. She cried: "But look. Why do I have to go through all that business at the bank? I don't understand any of it. And you do, Rick. Why can't I make out the check tonight, and tomorrow morning you and Mr. Swanson take it to the bank and do the whole thing?"

"That might work all right," Dice said. I guess I was supersensitive, but his voice sounded to me like a very small chariot with its brake set against the pull of four blooded stallions.

To balance it, I acted cool on the proposition. "I hate to carry a check of that size around," I argued.

I could almost hear Dice's teeth gnashing.

He needn't have been afraid. Barriers were only to be hurdled in Deb's exultant mood. She said, "Well, I needn't make it out to cash. I can make it out to you, Rick, and you can endorse it at the window."

I didn't dare look at Dice. There were times when my knowledge of human psychology reacted on him like an overdose of oxygen. I hoped to God he wouldn't burst out with a bad case of hysterics. I took the flashlight he was holding for

Deb to write the check, though. Its trembling beams were beginning to be noticeable.

She signed her name with a flourish. The ripping noise of the check coming out of the pad sounded loud in the still room. She turned to hand it to me. Her face looked like the face of a statue in the choir loft of a church. It had kind of a closed look as if it were straining to hold in a light too bright for the world to see. Her voice was a warm whisper:

"It's ours now, darling."

I knew she had no idea what she had said. I took the check and slid it into my billfold.

Dice was rubbing his hands and muttering. "That's fine. That fixes us up fine." There was an overtone of laughter in his voice. For a minute I had a crazy impulse. I wanted to hit him.

We drove Deb back to her house. At Dice's suggestion, she promised to call the bank cashier at nine the next morning and explain the need for haste in cashing the check. He would let me in the back door.

I saw her in. She was trembling still with that queer glow of exultation. She stood there a minute looking up at me, the moon throwing patterns on her upturned face. She said, choked, "Rick, I'm so happy. So terribly, terribly happy!"

"So am I," I said. I hadn't planned to say that. I hadn't planned to do what I did next. But my arms were around her. I was kissing her. And I was feeling exultant and warm and light. Intoxication.

It snapped me out of it. I didn't trust intoxication. My arms dropped from her. I stepped back. I managed to look contrite. I said, "I'm sorry."

She wasn't smiling anymore. Her breath was coming fast. She said, "Rick...." And then she didn't go on. She didn't need to. Her eyes were always a dead giveaway. They had the soft, bemused look of the awakened.

I didn't wait for any more. I said good night and went down the steps like a streak and climbed into the car. "Give it the gun," I said to Dice. As we whirled down the drive, past the hedge, I thought I heard her call.

"What was that?"

Dice laughed. "Hearing things? Well, brother, you ought to, after the evening you've gone through. Gremlins. We both ought."

Dice let the car idle along the quiet night road. He was jittery as a hophead. He was pleased with himself for coming in with me. Boasting that Silky had never given a sucker as smooth a play.

"Of course," he said with that dry cackle of his, "I doubt if Silky ever had such an easy mark."

"Shut up!"

I realized then what I'd been doing. Pushing off thought. Trying to hang onto that racing tingle, that glowing, senseless exultation I'd caught from this Clark doll. For a minute my mind was tricking me. Telling me I was the guy Deb Clark thought I was. Or I could be. Tomorrow morning I could take *McNulty* to the bank with me, I could buy that house. I could stay here in this town with Deb Clark. I could speak to coppers with no fear, grow old in a home of my own.

We turned a corner. A slice of moon-drenched Pacific showed through the eucalyptus trees. And my mind pulled itself out of its own mire. "Where," it jeered, "would you get the fifty thousand you promised to pay on the house?"

All at once the warmth, the exultation vanished. I felt low. Lower than I'd felt for a long time. One of those black moods rolling like a fog bank over me. I fought against it. I'd be in a hell of a state tomorrow morning to finish the play if I let it get me.

I said, "Drop me off at Tory's."

Dice was jolted bad. He broke off his happy ruminations to scowl at me. "You don't mean it!" he said. "You're not taking a chance of queering the play at this stage!"

I couldn't tell him the truth. I couldn't tell him I needed her right now. Needed her grasping, earthy realness to straighten me out, give me balance. I said curtly, "We're taking her with us when we blow town in the morning. She has to have a chance to pack."

Dice argued hotly. "How do you know Silky hasn't found her hangout? Doesn't have a tail on her? We'd be in a helluva mess if Silky caught us now."

"I can take care of myself," I said. "Pick me up on the way to the bank in the morning."

There was hate in his eyes. "Maybe I wasn't so damn smart sticking with you."

"Better make it quarter of nine. We want to have plenty of time."

The angry roar of the motor was his answer as he drove off.

I went across the sagging old porch and gave our signal ring on the doorbell. For a couple of minutes I could hear nothing but the waves on the sand, the wind through the trees, the rumble of an occasional car passing on the highway. Maybe Silky *had* found her and she had gone with him. A mink coat would probably have done the trick.

Then I saw a light go on at the back of the house. And in a minute the door opened. She stood there, tying the cord around her satin and feathered robe. Her hair was a rumpled mat, her face swollen from sleep.

"What the hell do you want?" she said.

I laughed. At that minute I loved her. The world had swung back into place for me. I felt the zest of the battle that was life, the tooth-and-claw struggle for existence, the exhilaration of the conqueror.

"Open the screen, sorehead," I said, "before I break it down."

She swung it open with a muttered oath. "I hope, for your sake, you've a good reason for breaking in this time of night."

"I've a hell of a good reason." I laughed and pulled her to me. She twisted out of my arms and slapped me. She walked backwards to a table and leaned against it, shouting at me.

"Listen, angel pants, I'm fed up with this, see? Sitting out in this dump every night listening to the sea gulls, while you paint the town with that society dame! If this is the only hour she can spare you, she can keep you, see?" Her eyes were blazing, tapering fingers closing around the stem of a cheap glass vase.

I chuckled. I couldn't blame her for being sick of this place. A dame would have to love a guy a lot to put up with straw mat rugs and castoff furniture of the golden oak, Mission era. She'd done her best with her motley assortment of kewpies, and lace pillows, but nothing could hide its sordidness. I started threading my way past half-empty liquor glasses, overflowing ash trays, and silk undergarments strewn over chairs and tables. I stumbled over a brilliant South American sandal.

I said, "Why don't you clean up the dump?"

She threw the vase at me. I dodged, and grabbed her while her arm was still up. She yelled at me to get out. I told her to shut her sulky mouth. She wasn't mad enough yet to tell her the good news. Might as well have a little fun first. I picked her up like a sputtering child. This did it fast. Fury raged through her. One bright-tipped claw went for my eye. I grabbed her wrists in one hand ... started across the room ...

When a queer coldness tensed me.

I had heard nothing except a slight creaking that could have been the wind. Yet even as I swung around, all Dice's warnings flooded through me. Silky's tail ... or maybe Silky himself....

And then I stood there dumb and frozen, Tory's kicking forgotten. Wishing to God it had been Silky!

Because it was Deb Clark standing there in the door, staring at me with wide, strange eyes that held in their depths the reflection of the room ... of Tory....

Her breath released in jagged spurts of words. "You ... dropped your keys ... in the hall. I called ... but you'd driven away ... I ... followed you .... thought you ... might ... need them...."

My arms relaxed and Tory dropped. She gave a yell of pain and outrage and started to swear.

I opened my mouth, hoping the right words would come. But Deb didn't wait. She hurled the keys in my direction, and the door slammed behind her.

In a couple of strides I was across the room. I wrenched the door open. But when I was halfway across the sagging porch, I heard the whir of her motor. Her car shot out onto the highway. Its taillight fled into the distance.

I cursed my luck. Not even my car here to follow!

I stood there on the steps feeling weak and sick. And Tory, from the doorway behind me said, "You'd better start the tale and make it good, baby. If you think you can two-time me ...!"

I swung around on her. I yelled, "You keep your goddamn trap shut. You just cost me a hundred grand!"

## Chapter 13

Tory stood in the doorway, her hand high on the jamb, the light flooding the voluptuous curves of her figure. Her face was shadowed but I had the feeling it was as immobile as the black masses of her hair. That her eyes were wide, staring at me in blank confusion.

Anger released her. She whirled and went into the house. The frail door slammed so violently it threatened to split.

I didn't go after her. I'd only yelled at her to relieve the pressure inside me. I could blame her, of course, for following me to Hart City. But no more than I could blame myself for coming here tonight. Or for trying a game on a redheaded woman. I'd gotten away with it once. But that's no reason for pushing Lady Luck. Any broken-down fink could tell you they're poison to grifters.

And the play breaking up over a measly little bunch of car keys! I dug my hand into my pocket. Yes, they must have been mine, all right. Dimly I remembered pulling out my handkerchief as I turned away from her to go to the car. That's when they must have dropped. Why didn't I hear them? I wasn't in the habit of dropping things. Of all the breaks!

The pressure was building up in my head again. The shack before me took on a haze that was more than the drifting hunks of fog. A red haze. It drifted over me, beat through my blood with sick, torpid fury. I had to move. To get away from it. I went between the dark, whispering trees down onto the grey wastes of sand. The haze followed, blanketed me. Thought and pain alike dimmed into a vast emptiness.

It was a long time before my brain began to function again. I was still tramping along the sand. My shoes were full of the soggy grains, my feet bruised and raw from it. The cold California night breeze had chilled me to the bone. My lips felt stiff, drawn back against my chattering teeth.

The consciousness of this physical pain was almost pleasant

though, for the pressure now had worn itself to a dark bank of resignation. My will was no longer hardened into bitter resistance against the unfair bludgeoning of Fate. The shock was past. The hundred grand—my dream of independence—had lost its sharp actuality. Its loss seemed less real. To hell with the dough. I never had it anyway.

A pallid dawn had darkened the ocean. Prisms of red and orange were shooting fan-shaped up through the mists that shrouded the horizon. I held my arms against my body and rubbed them with my stiff hands.

Providing I didn't get pneumonia from my night's outing, I thought, I was as well off as ever. I could go on with Silky as his first roper. All I had to do was convince him the fix had curdled through no fault of mine. Thank God, he had no way of finding out what had really happened. No way but Tory. And Tory happened to want me, not him.

There flashed through my mind then the picture of Tory standing in the doorway. Her confusion. Her anger. Tory was impulsive. In a fit of temper she could do fearful things. Such as going to Silky ...!

I began to run. I had no wind. The cold air burned down into my lungs like vitriol. My half-frozen legs threatened to fold under me. But I stumbled on, scanning the trees and rock formations with anxious eyes. Were they dimly familiar? Christ! If I was going in the wrong direction!

And then around a curve I saw the little shack looming in its shelter of trees. Reassurance came with the sight. There was no car there. She had no phone. It wouldn't be like Tory to start hiking in the middle of the night—and a cold night.

I went up the two back steps. Through the glass of the door I could look into the kitchen. My last fears melted. Tory was there, standing before the stove. The smell of frying bacon wafted out to me.

I opened the door and went in. I caught a glimpse of myself in the mirror hung over the sink, and was surprised at the slight effect the night's rigors had had upon me. The fog had left my hair a rumpled mass of curls. My lips were blue. It was devilishly becoming. I grinned at Tory over my chattering teeth.

"Your trick worked, baby," I said. "I couldn't resist that bacon." Her hand tightened for a minute on the handle of the skillet. She picked it up, turned around and slammed it with all her might at my head.

"Hey!" I dodged, and the wall beside me took the brunt of splattered eggs. Slices of bacon slid downwards slowly in the yellow mass.

"You get out of here. Get out and stay out! You damn, filthy-tempered cur! You....." Her scream cracked. She began to cry, sobs breaking through her curses, tears plopping off her chin when she stamped her foot.

I picked up the skillet, cleaned up the worst of the mess on the floor and carried it to the sink. I washed the skillet and put it back on the stove. Threw in four fresh slices of bacon.

She had collapsed into a chair by the table and was wiping her eyes with a corner of the tablecloth.

"Why don't you give a guy a chance to explain?" I said cheerfully.

"I did."

"Your timing was sour. I was a little cut up right then." I turned the bacon and broke eggs into the skillet.

"What did you mean I lost you a hundred grand?" she said in a voice that sounded like her throat was sore.

I stifled my laugh. I'd been out of my mind to figure she might go back to Silky. She was crazy about me. I'd never seen her cry before. She'd gone off her pins with jealousy of Deb Clark, and then I'd accused her of losing a hundred grand, a crime to her about five times worse than killing her own grandfather.

I took her plate to her and poured her a cup of coffee.

"What I meant was I lost *you* a hundred grand," I said. While we ate, I told her the play Dice and I had worked out for the Clark dame's sugar. I told her how it was to have put me in the bigshot circles where she and I wouldn't have to worry about Silky. How I'd come last night to tell her about it. I took the check from my billfold and tossed it across the table to her.

She picked it up, looked at it for a long time, her breath still catching on reflex sobs.

Then she said, "I didn't mean to talk like I did to you, Rick."

"Forget it."

"I thought maybe you'd fallen for that social ice pick."

I laughed. "Can't you see me living in Hart City? Boy scout leader and general pillar about town?"

Her glumness cracked under a laugh. "It would serve you right." She began to eat with more spirit, but her eyes kept wandering back to the check. She was feeling a lot worse about it now than I was.

"What about trying to cash it?"

I said, "Not a chance. On a check that size, the bank would call Deb for verification."

"A hundred thousand dollars," she murmured slowly, almost reverently. "To have it so near."

"Well, don't let it scorch your fingers."

"Maybe she isn't really mad at you."

"Sure. She's the kind of gal who'd overlook a little thing like you."

"Maybe if I went to her and told her it was all a mistake...."

I was able to laugh by this time. "You mean I stopped in here thinking it was the Y.M.C.A.?"

We finished our breakfast in silence. But that corkscrew brain of hers kept on working. By the time I leaned across to light her cigarette I could see there was something slowly hatching behind those green eyes.

She took a long drag and smiled at me smugly. "Do you remember when she came in?" she asked. "You were carrying me. But I was kicking and screaming. Well, just tell her you found me outside. I'd had too much to drink. You were bringing me in."

"Stop straining your brain," I said. "It's not going to last you too long as it is."

"What's the matter with that tale?"

"Nothing. Only Deb's not a moron."

She snapped spitefully. "That's just your opinion because she's nuts about you."

"She isn't nuts about me."

"Oh no? Then why was she so mad last night?"

"Because I'm supposed to be her husband's pal," I said. "And she can't believe her husband's pal would be less of a tin god than her husband was."

"Uh *huh*...." She sat there looking at me with a bright, vacant stare, shaking all the pieces around in her mind like a jigsaw. A cup of coffee later she came out of the trance with an exultant whoop. "It's simple! All you need to do is tell her I'm her *husband's* dame."

"That I'd just inherited you?"

"No. You hate me. Don't you see? I'd come to town to shake her down. And you heard about it and...."

I laughed. But she kept hammering on it.

"Her old man's dead, isn't he?"

"Yeah."

"Then why the hell isn't it safe?"

"You don't know what kind of a Christ-bitten sap this Clark guy was. Hell. Baby, he wouldn't look at you."

"Oh no?"

"No."

"Remember that towheaded farmer's kid in Hot Springs?"

She had me stopped there. That little jerk *was* a lot like this Jim Clark, and had he gone for her! She took advantage of my silence.

"You have all the dope on him, don't you? I could study it in case she tries to trip me up."

For a minute I weighed the thing. I decided it was too risky. I cuffed her ear playfully. "Forget it, baby. And if you ever want that little white neck of yours broken, just breathe a word of this to Silky."

She pushed the check across to me. "Put this in the note you write her," she said, "to show her you're on the up and up."

"I'm not writing her any note." But I pocketed the check. I wasn't taking any chances on this little piece of evidence ever getting back to Silky.

She was mad again. She got up and went into the living room. She was standing looking out of the fly-specked window when I caught up with her. She said bitterly: "Don't bother yourself about it. Why should you try to get any money for me? I don't need any. I can go on living in a dump, dodging Silky's tails, never going anywhere, never seeing anyone...."

I gave her a couple of hundred. "Go down to Madame DuBois in town," I told her, "and get yourself some new rags."

She went on pouting but she tucked the bills away fast in the neck of her dress.

"Remember the name. DuBois," I said. "You may have to pay a sucker price but it's safer right now than grabbing off hot goods."

"What makes you think I could get hot goods?"

"I don't know if you can. But if there's a fence in this town I'm damned sure *you* know it. Leave him alone, see?"

"Okay."

I was relieved. I didn't know whether she'd take an order with only two C's to back it up.

Dice honked out front after a while and I joined him in the car. He swung it around heading back to town. He was dressed to the teeth and still jittering.

I said, "Look, Dice. There's no hurry."

My tone tipped him off. He turned around. He began to shake. He yelled, "He did have a tail on her. Silky came out...."

"Silky doesn't know anything about it."

"Then what the devil ...?"

I told him about Deb showing up at the shack. His shaking got worse as the thing hit him. His bitterness took on an edge of violence. Dice was never one to take things easily. He'd had his hopes too high, he'd worked too hard last night. I saw now I'd have to let him down slower. When he began cursing me out, I told him to keep his shirt on.

"I'm not sure we've lost her yet."

"What do you mean you're not sure?"

"I've figured a way out. It'll take a day or so."

"What is it?"

I wouldn't tell him. He suspected my bluff, but he wasn't sure. I tried to shake him, but he insisted on coming up with me to my room. He meant to keep at me till I told him, and there was nothing I could do about it.

It didn't matter any as it turned out. Because when we went in, Silky was waiting!

He stood with his back to the door, looking us over with that cold fisheye stare he gets when he's murdering mad. But he waited till we shut the door before he spoke. Then he gave a glance over my packed bags.

"Going somewhere, boys?" he asked gently.

Dice went a couple of shades greyer. I pushed him into a chair. I said, "Sit down before you fall down, guy." I was stalling for time.

The minute was all I needed. When I turned back to Silky the tale was on the fire.

"We are," I said. "All of us. I started over to see you and heard you were here. That Clark dame has blown her top. We have to move and fast."

Silky kept right on looking at me, his lids half lowered over his eyes. His voice was level and expressionless. "Let's have it."

I started talking. I knew it had to be smooth to get by Silky.

I said, "Right from the start, Silky, if you remember, I didn't go for this returned hero stuff."

Silky's face tightened. He snapped, "I didn't come here to reminisce."

"Well, I walked into an elephant trap because of it. If you can tell me how I could have avoided it, or how to get out of it, the play's still on. Otherwise...."

He jerked his head violently. Silky hates persiflage when anyone else is handing it out.

I got into the lie fast. I had to keep his attention. If he looked around at Dice sitting there trembling, with that gaffed fish look on his pan, our goose would be cooked.

"It's just that the Clark dame wanted me to be speaker of the evening at the Veterans of Foreign Wars banquet."

I hoped to hell I sounded as cool as I thought I did. I couldn't be sure. There was a tightness at the base of my skull, a ringing in my ears. I'd known grifters who'd tried to lie to Silky and didn't get by. And Silky didn't look like he was in the market right now.

"You made a speech before," he said coldly. "Got a sore throat now?"

"There's to be an open forum afterward. A lot of guys who've been across asking questions. Of course, if you want me to take a chance...."

"Why didn't you talk the dame out of it?"

"Jesus, if you think I didn't try! You know twists. She only got more stubborn. Seems to think it's kind of an honor to that dead husband of hers. And she's a high-handed little bitch when it comes to him. It ended up with her yelling I must be ashamed of my record—maybe she'd better check it."

"Crissake!" Dice was staring at me stupefied, the fink! Before Silky could notice, I went on.

"I don't think she'll do that. But she'll blow off to her father. And he may do a little investigating. It wouldn't take much to prove I was tied in with you."

Silky was a tough customer. He made me go back over the story a couple of times, enlarge on it. But he didn't catch me up on any details. He had to admit finally he couldn't see any way out. He relieved his chagrin by snarling I'd lost my touch with the women.

I tried a little sarcasm. "Yeah. A fine mark she was. A couple of weeks out of the sanitarium."

He cut into what I made sound like the prologue to a long list of gripes. "There'll be a train leaving town in an hour," he said. "I'll give the boys the word. You and Dice follow with the car."

I drew a long breath. "St. Paul?"

He nodded.

When I shut the door after him, I felt like my troubles were over.

Dice was grinning too. He told me I handled that pretty neat. It didn't make me feel too bad to have an audience when I'd outplayed Silky.

"Now," Dice said excitedly, "the coast is clear."

"Uh huh." And then all at once I realized he wasn't thinking what I was thinking. He was still hanging on to the hope of fixing the game with Deb Clark.

I lit up a couple of fresh cigarettes and gave him one. I said, "Yeah. Clear either way. We can go along with Silky or take a long chance on this doll."

Dice began trembling again. He said angrily, "I thought you'd figured an angle to make it up with her."

"I did," I said easily. "I can make up with her all right. But I just remembered something we'd both forgotten. McNulty."

"What about McNulty?"

"He'll call Deb today. And she'll ask him about his trip and tell him about going to see the house with his Mr. Swanson. And he'll say, 'Who the devil is Swanson?'"

Dice was slowed, but he still had a little wind in his sails. He muttered there were always chances to be taken in every play.

"Sure," I agreed. "But a real estate agent calling his client is a chance that's too long for comfort."

Dice was clawing at his suspenders. They snapped back against his shirt with dull pinging sounds. He argued weakly. "Maybe he won't call her till afternoon. Maybe you could get it fixed up by then."

"Too many maybes there to suit me."

"Well, what if he *does* call her? You haven't anything to worry about. After all, she called *you* about going out to look at Seaview Villa last night. You didn't call *her*. She introduced 'Mr. Swanson' to *you*. And as long as I stay out of the way...."

I had to admit he had a point here. I decided to humor him and Tory both by making a try for it. I wanted to return the check anyway.

I wrote a short note to Deb. I said I was sorry she had seen what she did last night, and I didn't blame her for the conclusions she must have drawn from it. I said this was goodbye. I said although I hated to leave her thinking this of me, yet I preferred it to her knowing the truth of the situation.

I read the note back. I was pretty proud of it. It sounded like a straightforward guy laboring under a lot of emotion and imagining he was talking over her head. Only one thing worried me. This note would rouse her curiosity all right. But still maybe it wasn't pointed enough. What it needed was a convincer.

I was about to tear it up and try again, when the convincer popped into my mind. I ground out my cigarette and shoved the envelope into my pocket. "I'll be back," I told Dice. "Call a messenger."

I ran out the back way, cut across the parking lot and went into the pawnshop on the next street. The pawnbroker was a skinny little guy with a wilted collar and sad eyes, who sighed at every exertion life forced on him.

"You got any sharpshooter medals, Pop?" I asked him.

He reached a weary hand into his case and brought up a tray. I rummaged around among lapel insignias, sergeant stripes and silver identification bracelets and found four medals.

For a quarter he engraved on the one I chose: J.D.C. Jan. 5, '42.

I slipped it into my note and sealed the envelope on the way back to my room. It was a neat trick. I felt it gave the note a fifty-fifty chance. If it should work, my afternoon with Cotton at the boys' club wouldn't have been the washout I'd chalked it up. It was one more time I had cause to thank my photographic memory, and the years of training I'd put in when I was a circus grifter, memorizing the numbers on boxcars. That date under the vacant spot on the plaque of medals now. I hadn't expected to use it. But I'd automatically tabbed it. How many guys even on the grift could have come up with this one? It was one of those reasons I was where I was in the business. And why I had no right to stop till I hit the top.

Dice was waiting with the messenger. I gave the envelope to the kid and asked him how soon he could get it to the Owens' house.

He winked at me as he stuffed the bill I handed him into his pocket. "Six minutes," he promised. I could see he thought he was playing cupid, and I let him think it.

When he was gone I looked at my watch. It was nine-twenty. I felt a coldness under my skin. I said, "I told her in the note I was leaving. If she's going to call, she'll call right away. We'll give her till ten."

Dice objected irritably. No woman, he declared, could make up her mind about anything in forty minutes.

"McNulty will be in his office at ten," I reminded him. "He's a blustering old boy, and fond of Deb. It would be like him to throw us in the clink first and ask questions after. Remember we're playing with the city manager's daughter."

He quieted down some after that.

To keep him occupied while we waited, I tore open the letter I'd written to Charley Meyers and gave Dice the money to settle the bill. "Then go on to the garage and pick up the car," I told him.

He perked up. There wasn't a better man than Dice if you could keep a little action cooking for him.

"You might hint broadly to Charley," I called after him, "that I'm pretty busy right now but will say good-bye on my way out. I don't want him on the phone or up here blabbing good-byes if she calls."

While he was gone I polished off my bottle of whiskey. I wasn't nervous. In fact I was feeling pretty good about the way things were turning out.

She wasn't going to call. I was pretty certain of it. She'd had the note fifteen minutes. And I knew Deb Clark well enough now to know almost to the split second how long it took her to make up her mind about a thing. Just about ten minutes ago she had figured I was going away rather than tell her something about her husband. She was going to let me go. She was selling herself short rather than hear anything shady about a guy who was dead—a guy she had promised to love and to honor....

I'd never known a dame like her. I wouldn't have believed there were any. It almost made you believe those cock-and-bull tales those traveling minstrels used to dish out of women throwing themselves on their husband's funeral pyres.

I knew then I was glad I wasn't going to be the one to part her from those hundred G's. Even if she was going to throw them away. She was a hell of a nice girl and she ought to get at least that much fun out of her life. For my money, I'd rather play a mark who wasn't so damn easy. I slipped the whiskey bottle into my suitcase. I wondered if it was the drinks or if I was going soft about this play.

Lucky thing Tory couldn't hear me thinking it! I grinned. Would Tory be burned when she found we'd left her! But there was no other way. This was no time to take chances with Silky. I was going to have to be a good boy for a while till this failure of mine in Hart City dimmed a little. Because I wasn't fooling myself. Once we got back to St. Paul, Silky would have figured the angle to lay the blame on me. And he was still the big guy and I was the roper.

All I could do was wait for another chance like this one. And hang on to my keys next time. And hope Tory would be around again when it happened.

God, it would be hard to knuckle under to Silky after a whiff of freedom!

I saw Dice drive up across the street in my Cadillac. My watch said it was seven minutes till ten. Charley would be waiting for me at the desk. I'd need this time for good-byes. I picked up my suitcases and overcoat, any forgotten article, then left.

I had gone three steps down the hall when the phone rang back in my room. I knew it was Dice at the desk. I could go on. He'd figure I'd started. But I went back and picked up the phone.

I said, "Okay, Dice."

"I'm waiting for you at the desk."

I almost dropped the receiver. Because it wasn't Dice's voice. It was Deb Clark's.

## Chapter 14

I stood there gaping at that phone while the walls of my seven-by-ten room drew back and left me standing alone in a place the size of the Grand Central.

Through it rang the echo of her voice, so quiet, so pleasant, so full of dynamite. "... Waiting for you at the desk...."

Then the walls moved in again and I heard my heart thudding against my ribs. The receiver was on the hook. Dimly I remembered putting it there, murmuring, "Okay." I turned to the window and looked across the street. Dice was not in the car. My moving foot struck one of my suitcases. I picked them up and went out again into the corridor.

Each step was like walking against a wall. Something was haywire. Every particle of grifter sense I had was yelling. Was I walking into a trap? Were the cops with her? All the possible slips went through my mind. New York could have stooled to McNulty. Or Eddie Lukin, the crooner, had gotten to Deb. Even the guy in the pawnshop. I stopped in front of the window at the end of the hall. Outside was the fire escape. There was no one in the alley yet. I could do a fadeout there.

But with my hands on the iron of the railing, I hesitated. Deb's voice was in my ears again, quiet, pleasant. What if she had fallen for my note? What a sucker I'd be to light a rag with the cush practically in my mitt!

All at once I was convinced it was no trap. A soft apple like Deb Clark would never help set a trap. She'd be the one to warn me if there was one. She was crazy for me, I knew that.

I climbed back through the window and picked up my suitcases again. God, what a bull that might have been. I could have ranked the joint. My biggest fault has always been underselling myself.

I walked down the stairs. I hoped I didn't look like a man whose heart was knocking out the left side of his vest.

When I saw her, the surge of relief was like pain. She was alone, no cops with her. Only Charley leaning across the desk, his round pan shining with its habitual sunshine and benevolence.

A smile quivered across her face when she saw me, a smile with a touch of uncertainty in it, almost fright. I went across the lobby to her. I said, "Hello there."

"Could I talk to you a minute?" Her voice was still pleasant and quiet with that tremor underneath.

I grinned at her. "I don't know why not, Deb."

Charley exploded with laughter like I'd said something brilliant.

"You can use the game room." He rushed ahead of us across the lobby and chased out a couple of boys playing ping-pong. He beamed at us from the door. "I think you'll be comfortable here." He might as well have added, "my little lovebirds." He shut the door softly.

Deb had on a white silk tennis dress and a jade-green sweater. She looked fresh as paint except for the smudges under her eyes, and the look of strain around her mouth. She went over by the window.

Another girl would have done it because the light made her hair like molten brass, her skin transparent, showing under its whiteness the golden shadows of freckles. But somehow you knew Deb had done it because she needed the warm rays of the sun just now. Her hands were twisting the handle of her raffia bag. She watched a bird hedgehopping along a shrub outside.

She said, "I got your note, Rick."

"Good." I made it noncommittal, friendly.

"I don't quite understand it."

I laughed like I was embarrassed. "I guess I was in a hurry," I muttered. "Don't give it a thought. I'm glad you came down, though. I'd a lot rather say good-bye this way."

She didn't take her eyes off the bird. "Rick—where did you get that medal?"

Her voice had sunk a couple of octaves and all of a sudden I could feel how she was tied up in knots inside. I knew what my answer could do to her. I stood there seeing how her slim, tanned legs tapered down to neat ankles and white wedgies. And I thought of saying, "I got it in a pawnshop."

The thought jarred me out of my lethargy like a cold wind. Redheads *are* poison.

I said stiffly, "Suppose we just leave it that I did get it, and say good-bye, shall we?"

She turned then. Her eyes lifted to search my face. She said slowly, forcing out each word, "Did you get it from that—woman last night?"

I made a scoffing sound of denial.

"Did you?"

I gave her back a set stare. "The story of that medal is not mine to tell," I said hotly.

"You *have* told me." She dropped her eyes. Her voice was a choked whisper. She swayed. I thought she was going to fall. I put my arm around her shoulders. I could feel the trembling that went through her. For a minute I hated the whole business. I hated Silky who'd brought me out here in the first place. I hated her for telling me about that damn secret boodle of hers. I hated myself. Her bright hair was fragrant against my cheek. I wanted to tighten my arm around her shoulders, I wanted to hold her until her trembling stopped, kiss her lips until they could smile again, tell her it was all a game, a game only a bitch like Tory could have thought up to get that hundred grand.

Hundred grand.... I got hold of myself again.

"Look here, it wasn't as bad as you're thinking."

She began to cry. "It's like a horrible dream, Rick. I can't believe it. Not of Jim."

"It was the girl who was no good. I tried to warn him, but you know Jim. Bighearted, trusted everybody...."

Her head dug further into my shoulder. But she was listening through her sobs.

I said, "I don't suppose you've ever heard of camp followers."

"You mean girls ... not nice girls ... who lived near the army camps?"

"That's right. Well, this girl was a smoothie. She came to Jim with a sob story and he started in trying to comfort her ..."

Her body was taut. Her hands clenched. She wasn't sobbing now—or breathing. Christ, she *had* thought him a tin saint!

I said: "Last night I saw her on Main Street when I was on my way to pick you up for the dance. I'd heard of the game these women play and so...."

"What game?"

"Blackmailing soldiers' widows for their government insurance."

"Oh."

"So I made a date with her after the dance. I went out to that shack. I accused her of this blackmail game and she admitted it. She said she'd picked you because you were a big frog in a little puddle and your dad was in politics. She figured you'd pay plenty before you'd let her show the town some letters she has."

Deb's eyes hadn't left my face, her hand was hanging onto my sleeve. She said in a funny, flat voice, "Love letters—from Jim."

I nodded. "I'm afraid at that point," I said, "I went a little berserk. I started talking rough. I told her to pack her clothes, she was leaving town on the next train. She said she wasn't. I said she was if I had to dress her and throw her on board."

"That's when I came in."

"Yes."

"She was screaming and kicking. I ... thought she was just being coy."

"*To* the tune of a couple of ribs it feels like." I touched my side gingerly, then grinned. "Your seeing us gave her a jolt though. It put a dent in her little game, I was able to buy the letters and the medal. I burned the letters. But I thought you'd want the medal."

She nodded.

I looked down at my feet. I said, "I guess I'm not very bright. It never occurred to me you'd put the two together or I'd never have enclosed that medal in my letter."

Her hand tightened on my arm. She didn't say anything for a long time. When she began to talk her voice was low in her throat. "I know you wouldn't. You'd have gone away letting me believe you were a rotter and Jim was ... the great guy."

I took it up angrily. "Jim was a great guy and anyone who says he wasn't ...!"

Her voice wasn't much more than a deep tremor. "But he was human. And I'm glad, Rick."

I stared at her.

She was blinking tears but she smiled at me and gave a little gulping nod. "Honestly I'm glad. Because, you see—I'm human too."

All at once I knew what she was going to say. Her face gave it away, the tears on her upturned cheeks, the pliant eagerness in her body. She said it in a quick rush of words.

"I've been hating myself. Telling myself it was monstrous what was happening to me—falling in love with another man."

My hand moved before I knew what it was doing. Covered her mouth.

She put her own hand up and pressed mine against her lips, kissed it. I pulled it away. She smiled at me, and her voice was stronger. "But now I'm not horrified any longer. Now I'm only very, very happy that the man I picked is the kind of man he is."

I could see her lips moving but the words seemed to come from her eyes. "Oh Rick.... I love you so!"

My voice sounded hoarse. "Don't say that!"

Her eyes went right on shining. "Jim would understand. I know it—now."

This wasn't the way the play was to go at all. I tried to keep my head. I said quietly, "Look, Deb, you just think you're in love with me. Because I'm your closest link to Jim. And you're letting this silly girl business throw you."

"Really?" She lowered her eyes.

"Yes."

"What do you think I should do about it?"

"Nothing," I said, "at the minute. We'll go on as if nothing had happened. And you'll get your bearings again."

She lifted her head to smile at me. "I doubt that."

"Will you try?"

Her smile didn't change. "If you want me to, Rick."

I smiled back and held her hands in mine for a minute. I said softly, "Okay, here we go." And raised my voice to briskness. "Have you talked to McNulty this morning?"

"I forgot all about him."

Everything was beautiful again. I throttled my sigh of relief.

"Well, I'll run over and pick him up and stop at the bank and close the deal on Seaview Villa and then come by for you. We'll go out and round up a contractor and get started on the alterations." I began outlining our day.

All the time thanking my stars I'd got the check back from Tory. Talk about miracles! I could have laughed out loud thinking of the misery I'd gone through last night. Well, that's life when you go around underestimating yourself.

Deb was looking out the window again. She said softly, a little wonderingly, "Rick, I don't want to go on with the memorial."

I kept staring at her, thinking I hadn't heard her right. "Not now anyway."

"For God's sake, why not?"

"Because it'll make me think about Jim. I don't want to think about Jim yet. Maybe later when we come back...."

She looked at me then, and her smile was a funny little mixture of wistfulness and excitement. She came up close and her arms slid around my neck. She whispered, "You do love me, don't you, Rick?" Her fingers pressed against the back of my neck, pushing my head forward till my lips covered hers....

Shades of Winona Lake! Did I say nice dames were dynamite? Well, take a nice dame that's a redhead too, and you have an atomic bomb! Three kisses and I was on the ropes. She looked a little drugged herself.

"I haven't any pride left in me, Rick. Will you marry me?" she whispered.

I shook my head. "It's too soon." I kissed her again.

She said, "Oh, we'd go away. For six months ... a year...."

"What about your father?"

Her smile was enigmatic. She murmured, "He knows."

"Knows what?"

"That I'm in love with you. He told me what was the matter with me when I cried on his shoulder about seeing you with that girl last night."

A gong rang in my brain. I said, "Your father's back?"

She nodded. "He finished his business early."

Automatically I pulled her away from the window. I hoped to heaven Silky had gotten out of town all right. I'd have to lam fast.

But the thought stayed up in my brain when her arms tightened around me.

She whispered, "Let's not wait. Let's go away today. I can be packed in an hour. I'll leave a note for Dad. Oh, Rick …!"

I could feel her heart thudding, her body warm against mine. She did something to me—something not even Tory could do. All at once I knew I wasn't going to let her go.

"Rick, when?"

I was saying, and I couldn't stop myself, "There's a train for Frisco at 12:15."

When she had gone, I went across the street to the car. Dice was at the wheel. He leaned across and threw open the door with a trembling hand. He said, "I did a fadeout when she went by. Did you make it up with her?"

"Yeah."

He cursed his relief.

A bird swung on a branch just above the right fender. It could have been the crimson little hedgehopping addict outside the window. It tilted its bill and let out a full-hearted, rippling song. Leaves drifted through sunlight onto the hood of the car.

Dice's voice was excited. "Then everything's set?"

"Everything's set." And when I said it, I knew it was. It was something I wasn't going to figure on. It was just going to be like it had to be. I said, "Drive me to McNulty's. Step on it."

The starter buzzed. We shot away from the curb.

"And while I'm there, go down to the ticket office and pick up two train tickets on the 12:15 for Frisco."

"Okay, boss!"

"Get two reservations on a plane out of Frisco tonight for Quebec."

"You bet!"

"And a suite at the Hotel Frontenac for Mr. and Mrs. Richard Fagan."

Dice almost ran down six pedestrians.

I grabbed the wheel and he let me hold it. He sat there staring at me. Finally he said, "Is this a gag?"

"No."

"You didn't marry her?"

"No. I'm going to. In Frisco."

"But why?"

"Because I want to."

"With a check for a hundred G's in your pocket? She only has two hundred more to her name!"

"Look," I said, "do me a favor, will you? Drive the Cad to St. Paul and ship it on from there."

His amazement continued to mount. "You could have had that skirt in Miami with two million smackeroos," he said, "if you wanted to get it the hard way."

"That's right."

"Well then, for chrissake what's the matter with you?" He swung into the curb before McNulty's and I got out.

He said, "You know how Silky's going to feel about this."

"Sure. I know." I shut the door. I said, "Get those tickets. I'll find the car."

He slammed the Cadillac out into the lane of traffic.

I walked into McNulty's reception room. It was empty. I took the key of Seaview Villa from my pocket and hung it on its hook just as New York came out of the big boy's office. She winked at me. I could see everything was all right here. She was relieved I'd kept my word about the key.

"Is Fatso in?"

She giggled, and stuck her head back into his office. I could hear his booming assurance that of course he wanted to see me.

"I always want to see you, Rick Fagan!" He was planted back of his desk, his pudgy hand reaching out across it. "How are you this fine morning, huh? How are you?"

I said I was fine.

"And Deb. She didn't come with you?"

"No," I said. "Now we've seen all of the available locations, comes the hard part. Trying to decide among them."

He tried to hide burbling satisfaction. "Naturally. Naturally."

"I've about convinced her to get away for a few days. Take a trip. Give her perspective on her choice."

For a minute he looked troubled. There was always the possibility of a client seeing other property on a trip. His eyes studied me, slid away. Yes, I was determined about the thing. His jovial good nature returned.

"Wonderful idea, wonderful!" he cried. "Nothing like perspective when you can't make up your mind. And there's only one thing about this sale interests us. Seeing Deb satisfied."

I returned his smile. "Sure," I said. "And your ten percent." But I said the last to myself.

"Tell you what." He rang for New York and had her get out pictures of all the estates we'd seen. "Have Deb take these along with her."

"Well, if you say so." I frowned.

"You don't think it's a good idea?"

"No."

"Why not?"

"Because that's why I want her to get out of town. Put the whole thing out of her mind. Then one morning she'll wake up and she'll know which one she wants."

He said slowly, "Maybe you're right."

I shrugged "Send them along if you want to."

He looked at the pictures a long time, then he shoved them back on his desk. "I'm not sending them." He lit a cigar and puffed it slowly. He said, "That's the way to do it. I should have known it from the first. Sometimes when I've a decision to make, and get myself all steamed up figuring it out and deciding, then all at once all my figuring goes down the drain and I find myself doing it another way. Maybe a way I can't even figure ahead on."

I said, "Does it usually come out right when you do it that way?"

He scratched his head with his blunt fingertips. "Never exactly checked my averages. But it always comes out the way it's s'posed to, I reckon."

I let him go on for a while then telling what a great gal Deb was, and what a fine city manager she had for a father. I was trying for a little perspective on my own. He'd called the deal all right on the way I was playing from here. I couldn't figure ahead. I was a fool any way I tried. I didn't even want to figure for once in my life. Maybe tomorrow it would look different. Tomorrow I could figure it and I wouldn't be a fool.

All I knew now was I was going to Quebec with Deb. It didn't look like her father would make trouble. Even if Silky stooled to him, he'd try to keep quiet what he'd gotten into his family.

If the play went that way, I could always get the three hundred grand. There were a score of sure-fire methods. Or, you never knew, it might be when the time came around, Deb would hand it over herself to start me on my own. She had spirit, plenty of spirit, that doll. When she loved a guy she'd love him for keeps. Jim didn't count. She'd never loved Jim. She hadn't even known that till I came along.

I thought about having Deb with me at Quebec. And my mind stopped figuring again.

"You be around town for the next few days?"

I had to cover a start as I realized it was McNulty still talking.

"No. I've got some business."

I could see him wondering. But he nodded pleasantly and said he bet I had plenty of things to see to after being away at war so long.

It was hot when I got back out onto the street. The curb was lined with cars. Only two things to worry about now. That Deb's father would call her and she'd tell him and he'd interfere. Or that Dice couldn't get reservations. Neither one of these bothered me too much. Those chairs down at the city manager's office would be filled like they were that other day. And Owens would be up to his meek ears listening to every complaint.

As for reservations—if Dice hadn't gotten them, he could take the train back to St. Paul. We'd drive the car to Frisco and wait there.

I nodded to several people on the street, talked to others. Funny how fast you got to know people in a small town when you were a friend of the city manager's family. Almost like on board ship. Only here the voyage wouldn't end for fifty years or so. I wondered how it would feel to be a sucker. To know the same people most of your life. To have a family. And train them to be suckers. To grow a stomach. And know you'd die in your own home with your wife and your children and your neighbors riding with you to the cemetery, crying at your grave.

I thought of what they said of Coolidge. How would they know I was dead? I grinned. No, it still sounded definitely on the dull side. Even with Deb. And when I thought of Deb, I stopped thinking. I felt warm and light and happy.

The Cadillac was parked between two dusty, old-model sedans. Through the back window I caught a glimpse of Dice at the wheel. He must have gotten the tickets then. A surge of excitement went through me. Things were moving! I thought of McNulty scratching his white head and muttering, "It always comes out the way it's s'posed to, I reckon."

I walked faster, crossed the curb and bent to open the front door.

Tory was on the seat beside Dice!

I just stood there looking at her and my face must have reflected the jolt I'd taken.

Dice said, "Look what was in the car when I came out." He made signs he couldn't help it. But he didn't care too much either. He was pretty bitter.

"Hello," Tory said brightly. She tapped one turkey-red fingernail on a long box lying across her lap. "I've been shopping for the rags. How about a lift home?"

## Chapter 15

After that first jolt, the good news got through to me. Tory being there meant only one thing. Silky had left town. She'd never have risked showing up in my car on Main Street unless she knew damned well the coast was clear.

Then it was only Tory I had to deal with.

"Funny thing," I lied, "I was on my way to see you."

"How things work out," Tory purred. There's nothing like a new rag to put her in a right mood.

On my way around the car I glanced at my watch and did a rapid calculation. It was ten-forty. I had until twelve-twenty to get back to Deb's house. Plenty of time, if I let Tory out at her gate and didn't go in.

Dice climbed out and I slid under the wheel. "Wait for me in the lobby of your hotel," I told him. I raised an eyebrow and he made a circle with his thumb and forefinger below the level of the car window. He'd gotten the reservations.

He said, "Okay."

I knew he'd wait. He was sore at me, but he'd rather drive my car back to St. Paul than take the train.

The Cadillac swung out into the slow-moving line of cars, picked a nervous way around the laggards, stretched its lithe power along the Coastal Highway in a flow of easy speed. The sun beat down hot and caressing. A breeze straight from the cool white line of breakers on the beach beside the highway was refreshing as a vodka Collins. It was a good day. I liked everything about it. I liked the tapering line of Tory's arm as she fiddled with the lighter, the way her thick black hair blew away from her face, the full curves of her body under its thin sheath of tangerine silk on the leather seat beside me.

She was definitely a good dish—lots of chili, sometimes a dash too much of cayenne, but a thrill to the palate that could take it, and I could. Maybe after Quebec I'd see her again. After she got over her fury, she'd be waiting around. I liked to think of it.

I leaned back and got a lungful of the briny sunshine. "This

Western seacoast has something."

"Uh *huh*."

I knew if I wanted to drop her at her gate I had to keep the talk on an impersonal plane. The damn sunshine was too relaxing.

"Going to be a lot of business out here one of these years. Some lots along here wouldn't be a bad investment."

"No."

"Believe I'd get down closer to L. A. though. Kind of a good gamble this real estate racket. Guessing where the next business section is going to be."

She blew smoke my way. "You thinking of changing rackets?"

Trust a woman to find some way to make a conversation personal. "Me?" I laughed. "Afraid I'm too old a dog."

"Take my word for it," Tory said.

A white cloud thrust a fluffy finger across the sun, and in the sudden absence of the penetrating heat rays the breeze felt almost chill.

I stepped down on the throttle and the needle flipped further to the right. There was a hard core in Tory the sun didn't relax today. She wasn't the best companion for a leisured drive. Her shack was only a mile or so farther. I wasn't sorry.

She was giving a workmanlike imitation of relaxation though. Her head lay back on the cushion; she watched the smoke rings she blew as they wafted to the top of the windshield and met sudden death in the whipping breeze.

She said softly, "Did you send that note to her?"

"Sure."

"What happened?"

"Just what I expected—nothing. When a dame like this Deb Clark sees what she did, it's the fadeout. She probably didn't even open the letter."

She sighed.

"Anyway we tried, Baby," I said. "Even Silky admitted that."

"Did you tell him why she was mad?"

"Oh, sure," I said. "I said to him, 'Can you imagine that Clark dame blowing her top because she found me playing cribbage with Tory?' And he said, 'Well, well, is Tory in town? I must look her up sometime.'"

Tory giggled. "Remind me to slap you sometime."

I stopped grinning. "Silky was plenty hot about my letting this fix of his curdle before we had it in. I've let him down on this big idea of his, and I'm going to have to play dead for quite a while until he forgets it."

"Meaning?"

"Click heels, polish his double A's, come when called. We're leaving town today."

She said, "Oh. So that's why Dice was coming out of the travel agency. We're going back on the train and he's bringing the car."

I patted her knee. I said, "That's all I'd need to do to Silky right now, Baby. I only hope he didn't leave a tail in town this morning. Or this might be a fatal trip."

She didn't say anything. I saw it was going to cost me an extra couple of hundreds the way it was going now. But it was worth it. I took out my roll and peeled off the bills.

"Here," I said, "take a plane. Go to some town where you'll have fun while you're waiting. Because it's going to be a grind for a while."

She put the bills in her purse. I heard the snap of its catch as it went shut. But she still didn't open her trap.

I swung the car across the boulevard and pulled up beside the shack. It looked hot and dingy in the sun.

"Someday we'll come back and buy this place," I said. "A little paint and plaster and it would make a swell doghouse."

"Just a softie at heart," she jeered.

"Yeah." I did it smooth and fast. I said, "I hate like hell to say good-bye this way, but Dice and I have a train to catch."

She shrugged. "You're the boss. Only ... I was counting on a tall, cool one. And you ought to see my new dress. You blew me to it."

All at once I was tempted. After all, I had over an hour to squander. But I caught myself in time. Tory's calmness was that of a ticking bomb. She hadn't really fallen in with my elaborate plan of rehabilitating myself with Silky. Tory's constitution had no place for five-year plans—or five-month plans. She felt no responsibility for bringing about my downfall in the play, and she'd have no patience in building up my fortunes again. Tory thoroughly believed in eating her cake and having it too.

Right now I didn't need bifocals to see her game. She had made me miss trains before.

I patted her shoulder dismissingly. "Can't risk it today," I said. "Have to pack yet and kiss the town good-bye. Write me General Delivery, St. Paul. I'll be thinking of you—and how." I swung the door wider.

I should have been hep to her next move. Going around with Deb Clark must have slowed me up more than I knew. She started to get out, and all at once her hand flashed back and she snatched the key out of the ignition. I made a grab for her, but she jumped beyond my reach.

"Come in and get 'em!" She ran across the sand lot to her door.

I cursed her, yelled for her to bring them back. But she went in and slammed the door. Her laughter drifted back tantalizingly.

There was nothing for it but to go and get them. I wasn't too sorry. The wooden steps creaked under my weight. An hour and a half was plenty of time to get back, see Dice and make it to Deb's. God, why this sudden passion to play it so safe? Was I turning sucker?

She was standing in the middle of the room. She'd cleaned it up some, though she hadn't gotten as far as the ash trays. Her green eyes licked toward me like flames.

"You devil," I said. "Where are they?"

"Come and find them."

Thank God she was keeping it simple.

"All right." I started for her. Her eyes went on burning with that sulphurous glow.

She said softly, "You're a lousy liar. You're not following Silky. You're going to marry Deb Clark."

It caught me off balance. She said it like she knew it was so.

"Drop me off like a sack of meal and rush back to her, that's your idea, isn't it?"

I pulled myself together in the nick of time. I gave her a look of admiration, shook my head and laughed. "Christ!" I said, "I don't know why Silky doesn't let you figure the plays. You work out the sweetest nightmares!"

It must have been Dice, damn him! He was sore at me. He talked. Or maybe she just added it up from the way he was acting.

"Do I?" She shrugged away from my arm. She was being too damn quiet. I didn't like the way she was looking at me. "Then you're not marrying her?"

"You wouldn't be talking a lot of nonsense to make me miss my train, would you?" I said. "Let's have the keys, Beautiful."

The smile on her lips was screwed down hard. She said, "While I was trying on that dress at Madame DuBois' place, your redhaired angel phoned in. She had some things sent up on a special rush order *because she was leaving town to be married*. It was breezed all over the shop because it was to be hush-hush."

I swore silently. Trust a woman to break up the play for a few glad rags. Damn their vanity anyway! I forced a wry chuckle.

"Maybe she is getting married," I said. "She's the kind of coy tomato who'd think it would spite me for last night. And there's plenty of suckers in this town crazy for her."

"I never thought of that."

I felt better. "You never thought in your life." I chucked her under the chin with my fist playfully.

Tory's smile was still peculiar. "I was plenty hot," she said. "So when I saw Dice coming out of that travel agency, I went in. I asked the jerk at the desk for Mr. Fagan's tickets."

Her eyes moved over my face. There was light behind them but no expression. I got that tight feeling at the base of my skull.

I exploded with laughter. It sounded like the McCoy. I said, "Good old Hawkshaw. And he told you Dice had taken them."

"If you like yours in quotes," she said, "he said, as I remember, 'The gentleman who ordered the train and plane tickets to Quebec *for Mr. and Mrs. Fagan* just picked them up himself. I'm sorry, Miss.'"

She just kept looking at me with that lighted, blank gaze. I tried to laugh. But I didn't have the stuff. I couldn't even think of an out.

Her eyes narrowed. She went on, speaking slow. "Or maybe you're surprising me. You *are* taking me?"

There it was. A nice, satin gauntlet with the imprint of Tory's claws in the fingers.

"No. I'm not taking you."

My voice was harsher than I'd intended. A small line of white showed around her full lips, but she didn't move.

All at once I was tired, dead tired of this sparring. I came out with it flat. "You were right. I am marrying her." Truth was a luxury I didn't indulge in often. I let the words roll off my tongue in nice round syllables, enjoying them to the full.

I had a funny impression that Tory recoiled, yet my eyes told me she hadn't moved a muscle. Slowly it began to penetrate that something was really wrong. She wasn't throwing things. She wasn't blowing off any steam.

Automatically my mind called signals to block that kick. "It was your own idea that did it," I said. "That note brought her back all right. I lied to you there. But she was cold on the original play. Didn't want to buy the estate because it reminded her of this Clark kid and now she wants to forget him."

"Very touching."

"She had this idea of marriage. I tried to talk her out of it...."

"But your tongue was hanging out so far panting it froze."

"Look," I said, holding on to myself, "you want that hundred grand. You're the one who started this game. Now I'm playing it for three hundred. The kind of stake we could use to build up a real setup, get rid of Silky once and for all. Don't you want that?"

"Yeah, sure."

"We'll go to Buenos Aires maybe. Buy an *estancia*." She was so quiet I took the chance of putting my arms around her. It was the wrong move. She blew up like a gasoline tanker. She broke loose, fists flailing. The breath she'd been holding came out in convulsive gasps.

"You're not marrying that Sunday-school slob!" she said. "You're the kind of conceited jackass that would get lazy and go straight."

I was mad clear through now. I said, "Who the hell are you to tell me what I can do?"

She started to yell then, but I yelled louder. We'd fought plenty before, but this was different. She wasn't throwing things. She was cold and sarcastic with all her shouting. I wondered how I'd ever thought her beautiful. She was a cheap little slut. And she looked it.

But I couldn't let her down too fast. She could still do too much damage. I said, "I'll have Dice look you up in a month or two. And if you feel different, maybe we can get together." I started for the door walking on my toes. But still she didn't throw anything.

"Thanks," she said in a voice that was so small I hardly heard it, "but don't bother. I'm going over to the Vista del Mar."

So she *hadn't* known Silky was gone! She'd been in such a state over the ticket business, she'd climbed into my car willy-nilly. Well, my luck had held this time anyway.

I grinned back at her as I opened the door. "Save your taxi fare," I said. "Silky left town an hour ago."

Her laugh was as quiet as her voice. "That's what *you* think."

I didn't like it. I said, "What's the joke?"

She kept on laughing. She said, "After I came out of the travel agency, I called Silky's hotel."

The door swung shut again. My breath got clogged in my windpipe.

She let me wait awhile. Then she said slowly, "I caught him just as he was leaving. I'm afraid Silky hasn't a sense of humor when it comes to getting double-crossed."

The little bitch! I wanted to kill her. I started toward her.

She screamed at me. "I don't like being double-crossed either!" The drawer of the table beside her slid open. When she turned again, she had a heater in her hand.

A wave of cold fear washed over me, while the green slits that were her eyes measured me for a bier. But I knew the same instant she did, she couldn't do it.

She said, "I told you if you ever tried to marry, you'd marry a corpse." Her left fumbled into the depths of her purse as she moved toward the door, her right kept the automatic trained on me. She said, "Thanks for the ride out here to get the gun."

I stood there cursing myself for giving her that rod, my mind racing ahead. In the few minutes it would take her to cover the miles to Deb's house, I couldn't hope to hitch a ride to a phone to get a warning through. The scene flashed before me vivid as pain. Deb running down the stairs to answer the bell, that glow in her milk-white skin, in the mop of gold hair, that fire in the azure eyes, that excited smile on her red lips as she swung back the door....

The scene blurred into a red haze. I was conscious only of this fury, of the pounding, screaming rhythm of it as it moved my body to its demands. Tory's screams, the feel of her struggling arms, the cold touch of the automatic, were vague flotsam on the surging tide. The explosions were muffled, disappointing. My fingers clenched and clenched again. As her screaming ended, the clawing impact of her fighting body slid away from me. The thin floor protested under her weight. She moved convulsively once, was still.

The fury died out of me leaving my heart hammering through a body, that tightness at the base of my skull.

Slowly I turned my head.

Max's hunched shoulders half-filled the open window. Pressed close to him was Silky. Years passed before they moved. Finally Silky's cold eyes quit drilling me. He stepped in over the low sill. His voice rasped words heavy with hate.

"Fast worker."

## Chapter 16

I was chopped down with a hard left to the stomach once. Just before I went out I had a seasick feeling that ended in black spots edged in red.

I had some of the same feeling now.

When the floor stopped heaving, I went across and stood beside the kneeling Silky. I could tell by the way he dropped Tory's wrist there wasn't any pulse. Those tapering fingers with long painted nails were limp like I'd never seen them.

I couldn't believe it had happened. Tory couldn't be dead. It was a screwy nightmare. Tory was a raggle you couldn't think of as dying. I stood there, cold and shaking, watching the dark stain widen on the ugly matting of the floor.

Some of Silky's boys drifted in. Dimly my brain began to function. They must have been stationed around the house. Right now their faces reflected Silky's. They didn't like me.

I pushed the words up through a stiff throat. "It was self-defense."

Silky's voice rasped sarcasm. "Sure. With your gun, and the kid unarmed."

I'd forgotten the gun. I reached for it. He kicked my hand.

"Let it alone, you bastard!" He slapped me across the face with his open palm. He kept on slapping me and when I tripped and lost my balance, he kicked me. I had to take it. There wasn't anything else to do with those goons standing around itching to jump in.

He called me every vile name he could lay tongue to. He had an excuse now to work off some of his gorge over my cutting in on his dame, and he made the most of it. Lucky for me he wasn't the athletic type.

After a while he leaned back against the table and fought for breath.

I wiped blood off my lips, panted, "Can't take it, eh?"

Max's hamlike right moved longingly in the direction of his shoulder holster, but Silky didn't pay any attention to him.

www.ingramcontent.com/pod-product-compliance
Lightning Source LLC
LaVergne TN
LVHW021823060526
838201LV00058B/3484